THE LAST GARAGE SITTER

a novel by

Richard Curtis Hauschild

For
Clark & Carol

I wish to fly above the cynicism of my words
Like a plane bursting through a thick cloud comforter
To find the sun at twenty thousand feet, spoiled by nothing
Corona-collared pacemaker of the heartbroken.
Fill me up with all your frequencies
On every level simply free me.
Allow me to understand the motes and flares inside my
eyelids.
Let me read the signs and arrows through unmarked sky-
paths
And find again the soft green of my first backyard
Of the first house where I woke up to flowers
And fell asleep to winking firefly constellations.
The evening of life is innocence and a reunion with toys
It is the drowsy sensation of flying
When you rest assured in your clean, fresh bed
That birds never dream of dying

CHAPTER ONE

I was in a daze all during the two day ordeal that was my wife's funeral. The people I love had surrounded me to guide me through the parting, but I really didn't hear much of what was being said and I barely recognized folks who filed through the reception line. My eye kept wandering to the open casket where Pat was sleeping away her eternity. I am eighty years old and somehow I felt like a little boy, helplessly lost in sadness. Looking back I can tell you that there was no closure or relief even though I was told there would be. There was no letting go. Forgive me, but all I could think of was crawling in there with Pat and going to sleep next to her like I did for almost every night of our marriage. I wanted to feel her next to me. It didn't seem to matter that she was dead because now I figured I was, too. I spent the next couple of days in the garage dodging well-wishers and watching for her face in the kitchen window. That was hard because for the first time the garage beer let me down and made me cry. Everyone left me alone for a while. Everyone one except for the birds and they were everywhere.

Sonia Costello now owns the garage. She bought the place when Pat's daughter Carrie and her husband Mike convinced me that I needed to be in a place that could take care of me since I needed a lot of meds, special food, etc. to keep me alive. Hah, there's a concept! Prolong a miserable life. Well, I went along with it because I love Carrie and I knew it was hard for her to talk to me about the arrangement. I agreed with only one condition. While the sale was pending and before Sonia moved in, I would be allowed to live there and hang in the garage. It was going to be about four to six weeks and Carrie agreed. In the meantime, she and her husband Mike would be staying in the house.

So, I get my last hurrah as the garage sitter. What to do with the time? I have had a laptop for quite a while, but this is my first attempt at writing a book. Sonia and Carrie think it will be good therapy, whatever that is supposed to mean. I can only use one hand now so if the frustration of hunt and peck is good for my mind it is a mystery to me. I had actually lost the use of my right pecking hand after my second stroke, but I decided to do the physical therapy this time and it worked pretty good. I had given up on a lot of my bodily functions back then; it seems there are mysteries about healing that you have to work at. But, don't be expecting no Roland Heinz writing. I was his friend, not his protégé. I am not even sure I will share this with anybody, but one thing I do remember Roland telling me is that you write for yourself first. You have to entertain yourself, for cry-eye. Anyway, it is May, the best month for garage sitting; and I am ready to start; ready to begin the last chapter of my life with the first one of this book.

I'll begin with a revelation: Bim is short for Benjamin. Benjamin Allen Stouffer and no relation to the frozen food folks, although I admire their products. I hated Benjamin, Ben, Benjie, etc because some guys teased me about my name. Stuff like: Hey, Ben Franklin, go fly a kite. Well, I could never pronounce my name as a baby and could only say 'Bim', and that's what my family ended up calling me. I was born, raised, and lived my entire life in Fond du Lac, Wisconsin, which makes me a Cheesehead, a Packer backer, and a cheapskate. The latter trait came to the surface when buying beer. I was a Huber drinker for as long as they made the stuff and then just got whatever was on sale. Well, actually, I never drank any of that generic shit in the white can or that crappy Billy Beer from the 70's political scene. So why am I obsessing about beer in the third paragraph of my book? Because I want one, that's why! I only get one a day now because of the meds. Even when you're wheel chair bound and heading for the old folk's home you can't switch off your personality. I love beer.

And right on cue, here comes Carrie out of the back door with a can of beer.

"Hey, Beautiful." She is still one of the most gorgeous women I have ever seen. Lots of her mom in those blue eyes.

"You talkin' to me or the beer, Bim?"

"Both of you." I hope I am not drooling.

I will spare you readers the banality of the usual Q&A about how I feel. Every conversation these days begins with eye contact and a question about my health. Christ, I feel pretty good physically; it's just the mental part that hurts like hell. But, I love the family and try to put myself in their shoes. After all they are not putting me out on the curb to be picked up with the bulky waste. And besides, Carrie always brings a beer out for herself, too. She could have been my real daughter instead of a step.

"Molly is having everyone out for dinner tonight at Ghost Farm, Bim. Mel, Ray, and little Roland are staying there for a few days and she wants us all to get together. You up for it?"

Little Roland. That kid's name always made me smile. I wondered how in God's name that he could actually look like Rollie when his mom was Asian and his dad was Carrie's son. But, Little Rollie had those x-ray eyes like his namesake. And he always had a book in his hand every time I saw him.

"How old is that kid now, Carrie?"

"Almost eight."

I had to think about that. When you isolate your brain on a certain date in the past it tends to wash out all the years between then and now. I remember Melanie announcing her pregnancy at Christmas about five years after Roland had died. Now another eight or nine had gone by since then. How do you stop time? Well, I guess you can't so you just go along for the ride.

"Okay, sounds like a nice outing. Is Mike going to be around?"

Mike Gabler is still a successful photographer of the rich and famous, but even he has slowed down a bit. My guess is they had more money than Davey Crockett and were content to spend more time on their farm in Western Massachusetts. I always liked Mike, a sensible man and a good match for Carrie. She and little

Rollie were all that was left of Pat's gene pool. It's funny how you even treasure invisible genes and make them sentimental treasures.

"Mike is flying in this afternoon."

"Where has he been?"

"Mexico," Carrie sighed.

"Don't tell me…"

"Yep, another swimsuit issue."

"Well, if you ask me…"

"Bim," she said with that 'don't go there' tone that never stopped me from going anywhere.

"If you ask me, he can aim his camera at you and put the picture on the cover of any magazine known to man. All them fake boobs and puffed up lips don't do shit for me."

"Bim, you're eighty years old. Those boobs aren't aimed at you."

"Who cares what damned year I was born or how old I have survived to? Men age on the outside, but remain virile, powerful studs on the inside until we die!"

"I can believe that!"

Well, I got her giggling now. That is one of my talents.

"Wouldn't be that beer talking, would it?" she went on.

"Hell, one lousy beer never did no talking. Now a six-pack has a voice and a twelve-pack is the freaking Mormon Tabernacle Choir!"

"I bow to your expertise, Bimster."

I was about to give her another dose of my expertise, but I got lost in her smile. We both broke down laughing. My eyes shot to the kitchen window and for a second I thought I saw Pat smiling out at us. I took Carrie's free hand.

"I ever tell you how much I love you, girl?"

"Yes, but you don't have to say it because I know it."

We shared exactly one perfect moment of garage sitting and then her cell phone rang. I gathered it was Mike (unless she has some other 'sweetie') and I tuned them out. I watched the guy across the street mowing his lawn and wished I could still do that chore. I always loved the first couple mows of the year with all the violets popping up in the grass. I sort of hated to mow over them. I guess soon enough someone will be mowing over me.

Ghost Farm was Roland's place out in Pipe on Highway 151 and Molly Costello, his adopted daughter continued to live there after his passing. She eventually married a local veterinarian, Owen Palmer, and they set up a pretty good life for themselves. They called it a ghost farm because nothing was farmed there anymore, but everyone in the family knew the place was spook-haunted anyway so the name stuck. More on that later.

We've got the routine of packing me and my chair into the car down pretty good. I really never liked being handled by anyone, but a couple strokes change everything. I got used to being treated like a sack of potatoes, but at least I got to ride shotgun. I have made the trip out to Ghost Farm many times and in all weather and it never has ceased to amaze me how beautiful that place is. Here in May the forsythia dominate the driveway and the lilacs surround the house. It looks like the yellow barn got a new coat of paint since the last time I was here, too. The farm is up against The Ledge and looks out over Lake Winnebago to the west. No wonder Roland was inspired to write here even if the place doesn't have a garage.

Molly was waiting in the yard when we pulled up. I could see her smile from fifty yards away.

"Welcome back, Bim," she said with a hug. "We've been missing you around here."

As Molly greeted Mike and Carrie in similar fashion, I couldn't help but notice how lovely she still is, too, although she's now gone completely and naturally gray. As you may have noticed I still have an eye for female beauty and our extended family is full of it. In turn I was reunited with Molly's daughter Melanie and her husband Ray Hitowski. Ray is Pat's grandson and thereby my step-grandson. He is also a lawyer, which I long ago forgave him for. His father was Carrie's first husband, Crazy Ray Hitowski, the late, great (not my opinion) rock star. People say Crazy Ray put Fond du Lac on the map, but I would argue that Roland Heinz made that mark. After all, what is more important, rock and roll or literature? Okay, I lost that one.

It is a rather coolish day so the party is in the house. Molly and Owen have done a bit of remodeling around the farm, but the house remains pretty much the way Roland left it. Molly explained to me once that they did that to preserve Roland's memory. The place has become something of a national monument, I guess. Part of the barn has long been kept as a museum for Roland's literary artifacts including his two Pulitzer Prizes and I hear they even have tours come through from time to time. I am not sure how Rollie would have felt about that. He was a very private man, with few friends or fans while he was alive. I am proud to say we had a comfortable friendship over the years. I always say I knew him when. The 'when' part was not always so great for him, but it was magical for me. Anyway, he is out there by the lilacs with his dog. I wouldn't mind joining them when the time comes. Sometimes the dead can seem to be a lot more fun and welcoming than the living. I think about that too often these days.

Sonia, Molly's youngest, has just arrived and I have to admit I am getting a little impatient for her to get around to me. She and I have enjoyed a special friendship over the years: co-conspirators and black humorists. Finally, I realize she has saved me for last.

"So Bim, I see you are still alive," Sonia whispers in my ear as she hugs the heck out of me. She is a poet and philanthropist, a true diamond of a girl. Sonia was born in the Sudan and adopted by Molly, but she and her sister, who is Vietnamese, definitely were birthed by Molly's soul. Kind of like little Roland taking after his grandpa. Families tend to do that, I think, despite their varying origins. Maybe it is the pure goodness of this family that defines them. I love them all, but Sonia is special to me.

"Hi Sony, I'm dying alright. Dying for a beer." Old people make bad jokes.

"I'll get you one." She then seemed to survey my face doing some sort of African mind probe. "You okay with me buying your house? I'd buy you, too, if I could and keep you in the garage." Her dramatic frown suddenly bursts into a blinding smile.

"Christ, I wish you could do that," I said. "I'm trying not to think about Cedar whatever."

"Cedar Commons."

"Yeah, Sony, they use the word cedar to make it sound like the place smells good when it really smells like piss and bad food. But, yeah, I'd rather have you own that house than some stranger. Are you planning on living in it?"

"Well, it will be my home base when I am back here. I have always stayed with Mom and Owen when I was home, but I always wanted my own place in town. And don't worry; I am not going to touch the garage. It will remain the same for when you come back to haunt it."

I had to chuckle. Death really was becoming much more appealing than being pushed around life. "Just remember to keep the cooler filled and iced. I won't be on these damned meds in the GHA."

Sonia thought hard and deciphered me.

"The Great Here After? Oh, you really do plan to haunt the place?"

"Bingo."

"I'll get that beer."

"Good girl."

Roland Heinz Hitowski ambled over to say hi. Like I said, he reminds me of his namesake.

"What are you up to, kid?"

"About five feet, Mr. Stouffer. You?"

He was channeling Roland. Amazing!

"I guess I'm about four feet in this chair, Rollie." We shook hands.

"I prefer to be called Roland, if that's okay? What's it like to be in that wheelchair, Mr. Stouffer?"

"I prefer to be called Bim and the chair is necessary, but it sucks at the same time."

He thought about that for a second and then nodded seriously. Then in the same instant he smiled, lighting up my part of the room.

"Lots of stuff sucks. Life is tricky."

"Where did you hear that? I asked.

"I don't know, I just do a lot of listening."

"Then listen to this, Roland, things suck, but life is wonderful. The guy you were named after taught me that."

"Papa Roland."

"Yep. You gonna be a writer some day?"

At that moment his dad called for him to come and take out some trash, but before he left me he soft punched me in the shoulder.

"I already am…Bim."

I whispered, "Holy shit!" as I watched him walk away.

CHAPTER TWO

The tradition of nailing up old license plates in the garage is probably as old as the automobile itself. First of all, in the old days no one ever threw away anything made of metal. Secondly, each plate reminded the owner of a car or truck from the past and no guy ever let go of those memories. Old girlfriends and wives came and went, but the car was an old friend associated with good times. Mostly. I remember a couple of good fights that the first wife and I had in the car that the Wisconsin 1970 plate was on. That was the yellow plate with the black characters. Oh Geez, there were blue and white ones, maroon and white, red and white, and these newer farm plates that I never liked. As for personalized plates? My ego ain't worth the extra yearly fee, but I like the Packer ones. And these garage plates don't move with you. They stay where they were originally nailed so I got my second wife's husband's plates in my current garage. Sony will inherit my plates and that makes me feel okay about it.

I had some other real nice conversations and had some good food at Molly's, but I was getting restless. Here's what happens at these affairs: after dinner the women all go into the kitchen to do something they call 'chit-chat.' The men gather in the living room to do what they call bullshit. Now, I am the king of BS, but someone forgot to wheel me over to where the action is so I am still parked at the dining room table picking at a piece of rhubarb pie. I was thinking about making some noise when I saw a pickup truck pull into the drive. It took me a second or two to recognize The Irishman.

Every head turned to the kitchen door as Desmond O'Conner made his belated entrance. I should mention that Des was, isn't, and sometimes is again Sonia's partner and lover. I guess since they are both writers there is some sort of professional jealousy that turns their affair on and off. At first she was successful and then he was. It gives me a head ache to think about their heart ache. They always looked nice together, but who the hell knows what goes on in other people's lives. They are both international celebrities, or were at one time, and maybe that is a factor. Somebody is always patting invitingly on the bed for famous folks to join them. I suspect Des gave in a little too often, but maybe Sonia did, too. Des bought the old Bollander place several years ago, which is above Ghost Farm on the Ledge. Meg Bollander was a story in herself, but that should be the subject of someone else's book.

"Hello, Des, didn't expect to see you today." I said.

"Yes, well, I am back for a while," he whispered as he shook my hand. I noticed he was looking at Sonia all the while. "I just got in last night so…"

Before he could finish Sony arrived with a Miller Lite. I found myself right in the middle of what might be a family storm. I loved it.

"Hi, Des, when did you blow in?"

The question was presented to fit the cold wind metaphor. Writers.

"Last night. Sony. I was going to ring you up and then I saw all the cars down here. I am invited, right?"

Sonia shrugged. It was my turn to jump in.

"Well, for cry-eye give her a hug or something, O'Conner."

He gave her a hug for me, I guess and then they went outside to settle (or not) whatever had come between them this time. It left me alone once more and I found I had the time to make some other observations, the kind of things old people are thinking, but never talk about…because no one asks.

There was a framed portrait photo of Roland Heinz on the wall facing the lake view windows. I assumed that Mike Gabler had taken it. Then I remembered it was a blow up of the one from the coffee table book he had done when Mollie first came to Pipe to interview Roland. It was all coming back to me: that was the week Roland died so, of course, the photo would have great significance. Looking at this photo made me feel like Rollie was

13

here in the room. Something about that little shaft of light across his eyes seemed to animate the picture. Two Pulitzer Prizes for literature and a museum in a barn in Pipe, Wisconsin. That seemed out of whack although I knew his books still sold well internationally. In fact I read somewhere he was having a new boost of interest in Asia of all places.

Roland's most cherished heritage was probably his family. Yeah, Molly and her girls were adopted posthumously, but that was only a technicality of life. I had never thought of Molly as anyone but his daughter. He picked her, which to me is more endearing than some random roll of genetic dice. Rollie was a complicated man, but the love shone through. Or sometimes the lack of receiving it, I guess. When I read the book that Molly put together about his earlier years I learned quite a bit about my friend that I had never known before. Of course, I liked that book because I was featured in some of the anecdotes. Some reviewers even called me a 'loveable character'. I'll drink to that.

I am noticing that Melanie and Ray make eye contact quite often. It is like they don't want to lose track of where each other is in the room. It is clear to me that this comes from them having conflicting careers that keep them on other sides of the world more than not. Mel is a physician with *Caduceus International* and Ray is an entertainment lawyer in Los Angeles. She travels a lot to help the war-torn poor and he schmoozes with the well-fed rich and famous. Mel is Vietnamese and Ray is Wisconsin-Polish. I don't know what that makes little Roland except a real neat kid.

I mentioned Molly before, but didn't write much yet about her husband, Owen. In my humble opinion this guy is a real hero. He overcame a very serious attack from a cougar years ago that almost took his face off and somehow had enough heart and character to capture Molly's love. She could've had her pick of men around here, but she fell for Owen before and after his face got scarred and held on to that. She is my hero, too. She was also my wife Pat's best friend and God knows Pat and I both needed her during the cancer fight and beyond.

14

So this gathering is also my family. I get it that I am a minor member of the clan. I understand that I am the old guy in a wheel chair in the corner of the room. I get it that they think it is cute that I get my one beer and enjoy it so much. I truly understand that no one in the beginning or middle of their lives wants to hang out too much with someone at the end of theirs. My eyes find Roland again. What is it like Mr. Heinz? Do you worry about the things you miss?

I finish the beer and crush the can with my good hand. My writing hand now. And no I am not done with life yet. I just need to figure some stuff out.

Later that night I wheeled myself up the ramp that Owen had built from the driveway to the back door of my place. One of Pat's last projects was to fix up the den into a bedroom for me and she also added a downstairs bathroom off the kitchen with my comfort in mind. I navigate around the house using a walker so if I have to get up during the night (and I always do) I can manage on my own downstairs. It is strange sleeping in the room beneath the bedroom you used to sleep in, especially since another couple is sleeping in your old bed. Sometimes I can hear Carrie and Mike murmuring and wonder what they are talking about. I hope it is about their future and not mine. I have caught Carrie checking in on me during the night a few times and it makes me uneasy to know that she is that concerned. I suppose everyone will be relieved when I am in that cedar place. Everyone, but me. Now there is another chilling notion to have just before trying to sleep. Another day of freedom ends with the sound of the dozen or so house clocks mocking me. And then Roland comes to me in a dream.

There is a man picking up litter on the sidewalk and as I pass him I see it is Roland, but he doesn't recognize me. I stop right in front of him and he does not react at all. From behind me I hear a female voice that is calling my name. It sounds like Pat so I whirl around and see a large girl and then it dawns on me that it's Garnet Granger, Roland's most famous character.

"You thought I was her," she says.

"Yeah, I thought maybe, but now I know it's just a dream."

"Then why are you crying, Bim?"

I touched my cheeks and my fingers were wet. I had no answer, but Roland did.

"You got caught being human again, Bim."

"So you found your voice," I said.

"You find a lot of things if you look for them.

"Like what?" I asked.

"You'll see. Look for the birds…"

He then waved me off and he and Garnet went back to picking up litter. At least she looked back at me and waved. I woke up and realized I was crying in my sleep. I sat up on the edge of the bed and screwed my fists into my eyes. I wondered what time it was.

"Two thirty-five, honey"

It was Pat sitting in my wheel chair.

"Patsy? What are you doing here?"

"I am loving you, husband."

I woke up again when the door opened and Carrie came in.

"You okay? We heard you talking all the way up stairs."

I took a moment to clear my head.

"You know how Roland wrote about a dream within a dream?"

"Yeah…?"

"I just had one."

"Cool. What do you remember?" Carrie asked through a yawn.

"Roland was there…and Garnet Granger. And then your mom."

"Did they say anything?"

I shook my head trying to remember and then pulled one word out of my head. A word that was spinning away like a feather in a cyclone. "Birds."

"Interesting. We'll talk about it tomorrow. It's two thirty-five in the morning."

"Yeah, good night again, Carrie."

I was back in bed and asleep before the clock advanced another minute.

At breakfast, Mike and I were having coffee and trying to find something interesting in the paper, which is challenging these days. Neither one of us had said much, but then I guess the caffeine finally kicked in.

"I heard you were dreaming about birds last night, Bim," Mike said with a bemused look in his eye.

"Word travels fast around this place," I mumbled and slurped some spilled coffee out of my saucer. Even I didn't like my grouchy tone.

"Hey, Bim, I'm just trying to engage you. You've been a little distant since…"

"Since Pat died. Yeah, distant, like on Pluto."

"Let's start over. If I lost Carrie I would be out there, too. And if someone was sleeping in my bed I might be edgy at the breakfast table."

I, being the wise man I am, saw where this was going, that being nowhere.

"Mike, let me start over, okay? I dreamt about Roland and he mentioned something about birds." Then I remembered something else. "He and Garnet Granger were picking up pieces of paper off the street."

Mike tapped his finger on the table. "Dreams are supposed to mean something. Got any ideas?"

I figured this dream thing was not going to go away until I played this little psychoanalysis parlor game. What does your sleeping brain know that the wide-awake brain doesn't?

"Old Roland always used that catch phrase, "and everywhere there were birds." I think I read somewhere it was his signature," I mused.

"Yeah, I always wondered about that. It was in every one of his books."

"Hah, no mystery there," I barked. He explained it to me once. He had heard that if you ended up in hell you would know it because there would be no birds. In heaven the birds would be everywhere."

"Like they are around here."

"Exactly. He was trying to tell us we were already in heaven, Mike."

"Fond du Lac, Wisconsin?"

"It is for some folks."

I saw a light bulb come on in Mike's head. "Jah, unless you live in North Fondy."

It's an old local joke, but you usually only hear it from people from somewhere else. On that note I headed out the door and down the ramp for a morning of garage sitting. The weather had turned a bit cooler and I heard the distant rumble of thunder. These days a spring thunder shower passes for entertainment.

Left alone for a while gave me a chance to think about my dream. I really didn't want to obsess about it, but there was something bugging me. I know it is almost impossible to piece a dream back together unless you do it the second you wake up. A quick flash of lightning and the spontaneous thunder boom brought it all back into my mind as clear as day. It wasn't the bird message that troubled me. What I wondered about most was why Roland was grumpy with me and what exactly were those pieces of paper that he and Garnet were picking up. I love a good mystery, but this one seemed impossible to solve unless I could somehow crawl back into that dream. Maybe tonight?

CHAPTER THREE

Of course I live inside my head these days—inside my dreams. Where else do you go when you're done dancing? Since the loss of my wife, Pat, I think I have been trying to peek into Heaven. Since I was a child I have held a kind of picture of the place in my mind. You know, the usual green and clean place where everyone there is happy and all that. Now I am not so sure because I don't think that's where I want to go. I get confused with all this talk about religion these days, but it's kind of like, well I don't have to worry about taxes anymore so that only leaves one certain thing. Then I started thinking that since I missed Pat and would soon be evicted from the garage, it was my past that was my Heaven. I think sometimes I actually realized it and tried to take a picture in my mind of days when everything was perfect and in its place. That picture has faded away and will never be photographable again. I prefer the smell of old lawn mower gasoline and mildewed rags to anything cedar.

A few days into my current routine I figured out that it was not making me happy to be in the same place at the same time of day: kitchen table, garage, dinner table, bed. I brooded over it. What was I gonna do? Time was running out. I had a stupid idea I had been mulling over for a while and I needed to make a call for some help to sort it out, but when I ran down the contact list on my cell phone (yeah, I finally broke down) I could only find two people who I thought would listen to me without any patronizing hand-patting: Des and Sonia. I called the Irishman first and got him in his car coming into town. He said he would be by after his dentist appointment. He showed up just as Carrie and Mike were heading out for lunch. Perfect.

Des O'Conner was always a watchful man. At least that is what his body language was saying. I never saw a human head swivel as often as his, as if he was being followed or something. He pulled into the driveway as the other two pulled out and they waved. I saw white smiles through tinted windows. Then old Swivelhead popped out of his pickup truck checked his surroundings. Having assured himself of whatever, he plopped down next to me on a Fleet Farm folding chair.

"You gonna say something Irish like 'top o' the morning to you, Bim?'" I asked with a grin. I always liked to hear that bullshit Irish talk of his.

"Well, if that's what ye be a'wantin' then top o' the mornin', Mr. Stouffer."

"That's enough. Can it."

"You're in a mood today, Bim. Did you summon me here to berate me?"

With that he pulled two cans of Guinness out of his jacket and handed me one.

"Now that's what I summoned you here for, Desmond."

"I figured as much."

We popped our tops and toasted the day. I never thought much of this brown Irish beer, but it had a nice after taste that made me smack my lips.

"So why the urgent call, Bim? You sounded anxious on the phone."

"Well, it's not exactly any emergency. I just have some crazy ideas running through my head and when I think crazy I naturally think of you."

"I'll take that as a compliment, but only because I pretend to understand you, Bim."

"O'Conner, you're a man of imagination. I have enjoyed your books."

"Thank you."

"Your poetry sucked, but the novels are pretty good."

"So I've heard. You didn't summon me to give literary criticism, either. What's up?"

I took another long sip of that muddy Irish water.

"Okay, look I have a few weeks before the sale closes on this place and Sonia starts moving in. There's a pasture just outside of town that the family is going to put me out to."

Des nodded and sipped his own beer.

"I love this garage," I continued. "In fact, I would love to just sit out here until I keel over, but that would be messy for everyone."

"We don't want to make a mess, Bim."

"Right. But, Des, I want something else. I want one last…adventure."

Des looked me over as if appraising whether or not there was anything left in me let alone an adventure. I never felt more foolish, but that's why I had called Des. If he didn't get it no one would.

"Ah, I see. A little last fling before all the daytime TV and bland meals."

"Something like that, but fling means sex to my generation and that ain't what's on my mind these days."

"Okay, as they say, I'll bite. What?"

I had a folder next to my chair that was filled with print outs of articles I had pulled from the computer. I handed the folder to Des. Then I sat anxiously and watched his eyes as they scanned the papers. He betrayed nothing with his expression, which was good because I feared he might break out laughing. When he finished the last article he handed the folder back to me and then proceeded to go into 'The Thinker' pose, knuckles under his chin. Finally, he turned to me.

"Interesting question, Bim. Never thought about that one before. But, it seems quite a few other people have. Very interesting."

I had posed the question to the internet that if there were billions of birds around us all the time then why didn't we see more of them dead on the ground? There were literally hundreds of answers, mostly scientific explanations about scavengers, insects, and whatever. None of it convinced me.

"This is my quest, Des. You see I'm stuck here between this garage and a… damned dream I had."

I heard the choke in my own voice. I guess there is that instant when you sit in the witness stand to testify about your own life. It is humiliating for me to be so open with my thoughts because I have hidden them most of my life. Not the blustering snippets of bluff, but the dark ideas back in the corners of my head. How am I doing, Roland?

"Okay, Bim, a quest. What might you be questing?"

I was just about to lay out the stupidest idea of my life when I was interrupted by a truck pulling into the driveway. The passenger door opened and a young man hopped out. He was talking to the driver for a moment before walking up the driveway.

"Who's that?" Des asked.

"Must be the fella who's buying my car."

Here was another one of those closing moments in life. I had a '68 Chevelle SS 396 under a tarp in the garage and it had always been 'my baby.' Now I was going to have to hand the keys over to this kid. He looked okay, but I imagined this was what it was like to hand your daughter over to some stranger on a first date. He sure was smiling big as he approached.

"Mr. Stouffer?" the kid said.

"That's me. I'm Bim. This here is Des. You're the guy for the car, I reckon."

"Well, sir, I will need to test drive her first, but I'm the guy, yes. Billy Bondurant"

I recognized the last name from somewhere, but couldn't quite place it.

"Des, could you pull that tarp off the car?"

Now who doesn't appreciate a muscle car from an era where beauty and unbridled speed could be merged? She is dark blue, although I notice the paint has faded a bit even though it has been garaged and kept under the tarp. The kid lets out a low whistle and even Des looks impressed. Des leans into me as the kid looks her over.

"Jaysus, Bim, what are you getting for that beauty?"

"Fair price," I whisper the actual figure in his ear and now Des does that low whistle again.

"Here's the key, son. Take her for a spin. The gas might be a tad old so keep that in mind. Maybe put a fresh gallon of high test in to see how she really runs, okay?" I tossed him the key chain with the crossed checkered flags and a five dollar bill. They almost didn't want to leave my fingertips. The keys or the cash.

The Chevy turned over after a couple of cranks and the kid carefully eased her out of the garage. The truck in the driveway backed out and I finally heard a familiar roar as he hit the street. I listened long enough for him to get to the stop sign down the block and then I heard rubber. I smiled and looked up and saw those evenly spaced white clouds that look like sheep in a blue pasture and that triggered an old memory of the day I drove that car off the lot. It was the only brand new car I ever purchased. There is a smell associated with that feeling, too, but I just can't describe it because there is nothing to compare it to. Under similar clouds I headed down south Main Street to the frozen custard drive-in where we car guys hung out. When I drove that blue beauty into the lot I saw every head turn. One was a car hop I had had my eye on. I can only think of one analogy for some kid showing off his hot car that he had saved for: it was like have three extra inches on your johnson. I married that car hop, but that's another story with a nice beginning and a bad ending. Her name was Helen and it turned out she always liked that car way more than she ever liked me.

"What you thinking about, Bim?" Des asked. He was following my stare into the sheep clouds and wondering what shut me up.

"Well, that car brings back a lot of memories. You never knew my first wife. She was a real piece of work."

A statement like that produces silence. Des, God bless him, has those kind eyes that know when to just look at you and he lets you do the talking. I knew and he knew that we both had marital failures: those blazing new loves that flame out because sometimes love is more than air, fuel, and fire. I can still remember how I felt when Helen's best friend told me she was interested in me. It was the first time that I had ever considered adding a 'we' to my 'me.' It is so sweet for me still to remember that and then that dark cloud arrives. A loveless, childless marriage in this town back then was the ultimate failure. She reminded me of what a poor choice of a mate she had made until the day she died. That's probably why the car I loved was hidden under a tarp for all those years. Cars and women…fill in your own punch line.

Anyway, my car was now an antique being sold for money that would probably go to help pay for my funeral. It made me sentimental in the garage, a thing that happened more and more as time sped past me.

"Desmond, I want to tell you something. Something that I think about a lot, but never told anyone."

"Go on, Bim," he whispered.

I leaned closer to him to speak even though there was no one else in sight, let alone ear shot. I had not been to confession in ages, but here I had my Irish poet/priest in my gas fume and oil confessional. "I grew up on the west side of this town. The whole town was blue collar back then, but collars on the west side were frayed and tattered a little more. The trains moved through that part of town, cutting it in half almost hourly. They slowed you down during the day and woke you up at night. We lived right by the tracks near the river trestle. I looked out one winter night and saw a freight train passing a burning garbage drum and I could see the silhouette of a man standing by the fire. I don't know why, but I prayed for him that night. I prayed that he would be warm and safe. I danced away from those kinds of feelings when I got older. I have some regrets."

I wanted to stand, finish, and walk away; but of course I can't so I just levered myself up a little with my elbows on the armrest of my chair.

"All I ever wanted from life was to be safe and warm, Des. And right now I am feeling a little endangered and cold."

Des finally blinked his eyes and nodded. Then he winked that Irish wink.

"Jaysus, Mary, St. Joseph, and all the angels. All that I ever aspired to be as a poet just came out of your damned mouth. God bless you, Bim Stouffer."

We might have added useless words to the moment or I could have tied it all into my sketchy bird question, but suddenly Sonia Costello's Subaru was coming up the driveway. When you allude to angels, one usually shows up.

It was immediately apparent that Sonia and Des were in the middle of one of their "off" periods. These two seemed to fight often, which told me that that's the way they liked their relationship to go. If there was no love between them they would have parted long ago, but some people like drama. Sony hardly looked at Des as she walked up to where we were sitting.

"Good morning, Bim," she said and then as if an afterthought, "Hi, Des."

Des nodded and took a sip of beer as if it might have been a bracer against the cold shoulder he was getting.

"Good morning to you, Sony, I said. "I take it you got my message?"

"Yeah, got that and all the files you sent to me." She looked at the folder Des was still holding and nodded in Des' direction. "It looks like you got them, too."

"I did," was all he said.

I decided, since I had both of them here at the same time to lay it all out. Sony pulled up a chair. Des somehow found another Guinness in his coat and Sonia took it as she settled into our conference.

"I am taking a risk," I began, "by revealing to you how much senility and pre-dementia have already grabbed me. Birds have only become important to me late in life and mostly from reading Roland's books. I watch them come and go through the seasons from this garage. Some of them show up every day and you get to recognize them. They are important to me now and I just want to know what happens to them, you know, when they die…or when they are about to die. Where the heck do they go? You two are literary people so call it a quest if you want to. A quest for an old man who can't walk, let alone fly. An old man who wants one last damned answer to something!"

I sounded a little angry even to myself, but I knew it wasn't anger, it was desperation. Sonia took my hand. Her job was always to lighten me up.

"No, I do get it, Bim. I spent last night on the computer doing some research. You have a valid as well as a romantic question. If there is an answer out there we will find it, okay?"

"What's your plan?" I asked.

"I found a few chat rooms and forums for birdwatchers, ornithologists, any people who are bird enthusiasts. I went local and international so we'll see if anyone wants to share information on avian thanatology."

"Big words, Sonia," said Des with a smile. She almost returned it.

"Do you have any ideas, Des?" she asked. Even I knew that was a loaded question.

"Well, I just got in on this today," he said, "let me think it over. Anyway, you're a better researcher than I, love."

Funny how that word worked its way into this discussion. At least it got them to make eye contact. Sonia nodded, but still didn't return his smile. She then excused herself promising to call me when something turned up. Des and I watched her back out of the driveway just before the Chevelle pulled back in. I am going to skip some car talk here and cut to the chase. I got a cashier's check for the car, signed over the title, and it was gone forever. It made me unsettled, but heck, I knew it was coming. To help put it past me I re-engaged Des.

"Okay, now that my car is history maybe you can fill me in on what's up between you and Sonia."

"I was hoping you weren't going to ask that question."

"That bad, huh? There's a bottle of Jameson back behind that tool box. I keep it like you keep a fire extinquisher: break open only in case of emergency."

He thought about it, but declined.

"Shit, Bim, I met a woman in New York who works for my publisher and, well some stuff got into the gossip grape vine and…you know. Sonia jumped to conclusions. You're looking at an innocent man."

I put my hand up in a halt gesture. "Enough, Irishman. Heard it all before. When are you two going to stop this crap and settle down? This family needs a wedding sometime before it has another funeral, namely mine."

"I hear you, Bim."

"Work on it then."

"Would that be a last request of a sort?"

"Just good advice from a friend. I don't want you or her to end up where I am with a bunch of false teeth and regrets. Kapeesh? (I don't know how to spell it, but I like the word).

"Yeah," he said sheepishly.

"Good, then wheel me into the house. I gotta eliminate some of that Irish rust water."

I not only love those kids and want them to be happy, but I need to keep my bird team together for a few weeks. I spent a dreamless night, which I actually don't like. Sleeping without dreams is maybe too much like what is just around the bend for me.

CHAPTER FOUR

When I was a kid if you weren't any good at sports, which I was not, you naturally became a 'hard guy.' Hard guys were broken down into car guys and motorcycle guys. Those groups had their subsets, too, like muscle cars vs. vintage cars and Harley-Davidson guys vs. the dirt bike guys. One thing we all had in common was a little grease in the hair and dirt under the fingernails. It was also pretty standard to roll your cigarette pack up your t-shirt sleeve. Tattoos were okay, but they were much rarer back then than they are today. Geez, when I see a pretty girl all marked up I wonder what the world is coming to, but then I have to remind myself that my dad was always saying that, which checkmates me. So okay, now my car is gone out of the garage, you can't put grease on a bald head, and I quit smoking when my wife, Pat told me I had to quit when she did. By the way, both of my wives died of cancer and both smoked like chimneys. I couldn't afford the habit anymore, anyway, anyhow. So now the question is how do I maintain my hard guy persona and become interested in birds at the same time. I guess I'll just hide behind my age and watch everyone smile and nod that old Bim is a doddering fool and must be indulged. Or maybe I will call a cab and go downtown and get a bird tattoo. I saw one once that had an eagle with a snake in its mouth. That might work. You can stop laughing at the end of this paragraph.

I hadn't heard a word from the bickering duo, Sony and Des for a couple days and was starting to think my idea was being brushed off. On Saturday afternoon Melanie and Ray were supposed to come over and take me to this Cedar Commons prison camp to take a look at my cell. I waited for them in the garage and figured I could either make it a miserable trip or make the best of a ride in the country. I ended up flipping a coin (several times) and acting cheerful won the day. When I saw that Little Roland was coming along I knew I had made the right choice.

My future residence (their word) is out in the country; in fact it was smack dab in the middle of the Holyland between St. Cloud and Mt.Calvary. This was my first visit in person although I had seen their brochure. My first impression was that I was being taken to the funny farm, complete with a barn and silo. There were animals all over the grounds, too, like a petting zoo. A future filled with screaming peacocks and mewling barn cats was not my idea of fun until we got inside and I saw the other side of the coin.

I should have been prepared for a place filled with old people in wheelchairs, but it stunned me to see so many folks just like me. Well, not exactly just like me because as we all know, I really didn't belong there. I was just going along with the family will. And that is as fine a piece of bullshit that I have ever come up with, but I humor myself from time to time. I noticed Roland was a bit put off by the spectacle, too, so I leaned into him while Melanie went to find the warden, I mean superintendent.

"What do you make of this place, Roland?"

He looked at me with a furrowed brow. "Everyone is on wheels," he said, stating the obvious.

"Yeah, just like me."

"No, I mean I thought someone might be just walking around."

I said, "Look at it this way, if they could walk around they would probably walk out of here and you wouldn't see them."

He thought that prospect over and then smiled. "If they could walk they probably wouldn't be here in the first place."

Now I was starting to get depressed, but the kid hit me with an afterthought that seemed to be a whisper from his namesake: "I'll bet a lot of these people did amazing things when they were younger, right?"

Sometimes when you sigh you inhale a tiny mote of the wisdom of humanity. I tasted it and it was as sweet as clover honey from an Amish roadside stand. I settled my mind to what was to come next or at least soon. I was not going to be joining a leper colony, but rather taking my place among my peers:

storytellers who only had their own life stories left to tell. Roland stuck by me that afternoon, the kid and the friendly ghost of the same name.

While Roland and Ray took a tour of the barn and animal pens, Mel and I had a chance to talk alone. I couldn't remember the last time that had happened. Everyone in the family knew that her sister and I had a special relationship, but that was mostly because Sonia and I saw each other more often. Melanie's career as an international relief physician kept her away from Wisconsin for most months of the year. She had always seemed to be a little aloof when she was around, but I just figured she had a lot on her mind. Somehow today she seemed to be more relaxed, warmer. I looked forward to finding out why.

"Do you really think this is going to be okay for you, Bim?"

I must have looked confused so she put it another way. "Do you think you can make the best out of living here?"

My only hesitation was caused by getting lost in her eye contact. "Mel, don't worry about me. I understand all of this. Nobody wants to get to this point, but I am resigned to it. Besides, if I cause a fuss no one will ever come out here to see me, right?"

She smiled: brown eyes like dark chocolate and teeth as white as the first snow. "I would always come to visit even if you were acting like an asshole, Bimster."

"Hah, I thought your sister had the smart mouth trait all to herself."

"It runs in the family."

I watched Roland and Ray getting friendly with white tail fawn and then turned back to Mel. "That son of yours is something else."

"I hear that a lot, but I know you see Papa in him like I do."

"Yeah, how does that work? I mean…you know."

"All I can say is we are a weird family coming from so many cultures and interests. Genetics don't totally control people and my son is definitely, as you say, something else."

She started laughing, a sound I had never heard before. It caught me off guard.

"Melanie, you are actually giggling."

She made a face and stuck her tongue out at me. "Yeah, so what?"

"What else is going on?"

She looked at her husband and son and nodded at them. "Ray and I have made a decision and you might as well be the first to know. Ray is leaving LaLa Land and is taking a position with Pat Zeneb's old law firm in Fond du Lac. We're selling our condo in L.A."

"And you?"

"I am retiring from *Caduceus International* and going into private practice here, too. I am going to become a country doctor and probably work out of Owen's office at the farm. We are buying a place down on the lake near Calumetville. Is that enough news for you?"

It was, but I needed a little more. "Why?"

"We think our son needs to have a stable place to finish growing up. He just turned eight and has been everywhere already. Los Angeles is too big; the world is too vast and dangerous. We think Wisconsin is perfect so we're coming home for good."

Great, I thought. Just as I'm checking out of the Hotel Wisconsin everyone else is checking in. "That is very good news, honey."

We finally met with the superintendent of the place and she showed me where I would be living and a little bit of how things worked there. Besides the dogs roaming the halls (which I thought was a huge perk) I noticed that there were lots of bird cages in the common areas. This created a subliminal chirping gaiety that had a calming effect. I made a mental note of getting to know the dogs and birds as soon as I moved in. Some of the humans frightened me a little. Dementia is the worst part of this type of community living. I worried that I might begin to slip into it someday. Typical fears, I guess.

On the way home Roland quizzed me about what I did before I retired.

"Well, son, I had a few jobs. I worked in the quarry with your Papa Roland for a few years until my hearing failed. Then I worked in a factory doing close work until my eyes failed. Then I went into business for myself selling insurance to suckers until the economy failed. Luckily, I was close enough to retirement age when that happened and I became a garage sitter."

Mel and Ray both gave me 'that' look like I was holding a can of worms in one hand and a can opener in the other.

"What exactly is a garage sitter?" Roland asked.

"That's a good question," I said as my mind mentally reached for a beer. "I think it has something to do with getting out of the house without leaving the house."

Roland cocked his head.

"Okay, some guys don't want to be inside with the soap operas, the phone ringing, and the other stuff that goes on in there. In my case, I was originally going to the garage to escape the scorn of my first wife."

"Bim…" warned Melanie.

"Then by the time I married Pat it was just a habit. The garage was merely my space. All were welcomed, but it was my territory. You get that, right?"

"I have seen guys all over town sitting in their garages," said Ray, "I never thought much about it, but hey I met you in the garage, right?"

"I remember that day vividly," I said. "Didn't like you much at first sight."

"But, you warmed up later." Ray reached over and tapped my leg.

"You turned out okay, Ray, but…"

I stopped myself. I realized I was trying to explain things that I have never really thought through before. I had no idea why I hung out in the garage and neither did any of the other local idiots who did the same thing all their lives. I had no bad first impression of Ray Hitowski, except that I didn't know who he was at first. I was trying to impress Roland with a story that had no beginning or ending. I felt my jaw tighten as I clamped it shut. What I was really feeling deep down inside was how boring I was sounding. This was the heart of the matter of me at 80 years old. I was losing the ability to be interesting even to myself. I was canned, as they used to say. And that was another thing: "they" used to say too many things before "they" just freakin' died.

"But, what, Bim? You were saying," said Ray.

"Wasn't important. I lost my train of thought."

Thank God before someone nervously mentioned the senior moment line my cell phone chimed and the caller I.D. said it was Sonia. She said she had found something interesting about the bird thing. That's what it was referred to now: the bird thing. I told her I would call her back when I got back to the garage.

When I hung up Melanie said, "What bird thing?"

I felt everyone looking at me, which made me uncomfortable.

"It's nothing," I said, but it was suddenly everything.

CHAPTER FIVE

Meanwhile, back in the garage. Eventually, I did come up with a better theory for the garage sitting phenomenon. It is obvious to me now that deep within the embedded psyche of man is the urge to return to sitting in the mouth of the prehistoric cave that we emerged from. Long before the house was invented the garage/cave was already there. Well, it's a theory, anyway. I also recognize that there are sub-sets of garage sitters. First of all, I am one of the purists. A folding lawn chair, a small cooler, and a newspaper are my only personal requirements for a day of sitting. It seems some of my cohorts around town are not as Spartan with their comforts. I have seen some garages decorated like a guest room complete with a couch and cable TV. I have also seen what I call the board room garage with seating for up to a half a dozen cronies that spills out into the driveway. No, you have to keep it in the mouth of the cave, behind the line where the door comes down to the driveway. And some of the local garages are just too damned neat. I am personally offended by men who have to have a drawer or a hook for every damned thing in the garage. Shelves do the job just fine. Old shelves with stains and character. These plastic drawer things from the big box stores are simply not cave-like. And one last thing about decoration: I have nothing against drawing stick men and animals on the walls like the old guys or maybe a girly calendar from the auto supply store, but, you don't hang a framed painting or a print in the garage unless it is of Bart Starr.

I was waiting for Sonia to come over with her "news" and passing the time going through a couple boxes of junk that hadn't seen the light of day in years. I asked Carrie to build me a little fire in the grill for the purpose of their destruction. When she asked me why I had to burn old papers I told her it was just an odd obsession I had about keeping the past in the past. She was dubious by her look, but left me alone with the fire.

I was burning some old, embarrassing court records, which tripped an interesting memory. Back in the day, me and my buddies, Gene and Eddie were out cruising Main Street one steamy summer night in my Chevy. Eddie had a couple of six packs in the back seat that he was dispensing to me and Gene. Drinking was no big thing back then because the whole town was running on beer on weekends. Anyway, we pulled into the Clark station to get some smokes and Eddie volunteers to run in. A few seconds later he hops back into the back seat and yells for me to step on it. The rest is a bit blurry, but to make a long story short, Eddie bought cigarettes and then decided he would include a little armed robbery in the transaction.

I knew Eddie carried a gun back then so he could act tougher than he was. I also knew it was never loaded. Why he pulled it on the gas station attendant I will never know, but it only took about five minutes for the police to pull us over and make arrests. I got off easy with only a couple of days in the county jail for being an unknowing accessory after the fact or some such mumbo jumbo. Eddie got three years in Waupun and Gene got a big laugh out of the whole thing. Anyway, the reason I am even mentioning this story is because that's the night I became friends with Roland Heinz...in jail!

Roland wasn't a town guy. He was from some farm out in the sticks, but I had seen him around from time to time. He and I both worked at the quarry for a while, but on different shifts so we were just nodding acquaintances. I actually trained him for a couple days when he was fresh out of the army. He was a nice guy, but distant. On that night he looked like crap and I could smell the alcohol coming out of his pores. I was nervous about being locked up and wanted to talk to someone.

"Hi, you probably don't remember me," I said to break the ice.

Roland looked me over and nodded his head.

"No, I remember you from the quarry. You have a funny name."

"It's Bim. Bim Stouffer."

"Yeah, I'm Roland Heinz. You still work there?"

"Not since last spring. The blasting blew my ears out."

"It'll do that. You didn't wear protection?"

"Always forgot the plugs. I take it you ain't there anymore."

"Naw, I left…I don't know…a while ago."

"What got you in here, Roland?"

"Life."

"Huh?"

"Divorce. Couldn't ever get over the war. Can't sleep without drinking. That kind of stuff will always get you in here eventually. What about you?"

I was still thinking how life could get you in jail. I knew it was true, but it seemed funny to hear it from some guy I always thought had it together.

"I was in the wrong place at the wrong time," I said trying to sound innocent and witty. Roland just smiled and looked away. Far away.

Anyway, from that day we sort of kept running into each other. Mostly in Main Street bars. We were both trying to forget our wives only I was still living with mine. On some of those occasions he would tell me some pretty spooky stories about what went on in Viet Nam. I never got drafted because of my hearing loss. I should report that my hearing partially returned a couple years after I left the quarry. I don't know how that happened, but it stuck around long enough to keep me out of the army. Things like that are hard to figure. My dad always said the Stouffers were fast healers. We did each other a few favors, listened to each other's griping, and became friends. We stayed in touch through the years even though he disappeared for some of them. I found out later what he was up to and that part amazes me even to this day. Who knew I would share a jail cell with a two-time Pulitzer Prize winner?

I had just tossed the last nasty piece of my past into the flames when Sonia arrived.

"Don't tell me," she said, "burning the family secrets."

Like I said before, we are tuned into each other.

"It's not quite like that, but I hate to leave little bits of gossip behind. Some things that you do when you were a kid are not meant for future speculation."

"What'd you do, Bim, rob a bank?"

I closed one eye like a pirate. "It was a gas station and I didn't do the robbing. I drove the getaway car, but didn't know I was doing it. Long story. Anyway, that, in a round-about way is how me and Roland got to be friends."

"Papa robbed a gas station?"

This is exactly why I was burning this stuff.

"He had nothing to do with it. I met him in jail."

Sonia's eyebrows shot to her forehead. Again, this is why you burn the past.

"Oh shit, Sony, your Papa was no saint back in the old days. You already knew that from his own writing."

I saw an opening to pivot. "You said on the phone you had something interesting…?

I watched her mind go from jail cell to bird cage.

"Yes, maybe. You got a few minutes?"

There was a brief moment of ironic silence and then we both laughed at my thousands of available minutes. Evening comes early and lasts longer this time of year and the sky was already rosy in the west and indigo in the east. It was almost dinner time in town and the traffic on the street was infrequent. I wished the little fire was hotter to take the chill out of the air, but then Sonia had a little fire in her dark eyes and that was enough for now.

"See if you can follow this," she began. "Last night I went back to some of the chat rooms where I had posed our question and it was mostly ignored. Either that or some birders gave the usual explanations about predators, insects, etc. But, not everyone."

"You found one kook like me, eh?"

"Well, Bim, let's just say I found someone. You wanna go inside? You look cold."

"In a minute. You can't leave me hanging."

"Okay, I found this guy and we went back and forth in this birder chat room. When I asked some specific questions he suggested we do a private chat so we went to a private chat room."

"Sony, can you cut the web mumbo jumbo? I have no idea what you're talking about."

"Okay, yeah, bottom line. This guy is a Native American and he lives not too far from here in a little place called Quinney. He said he had some information that might be interesting, but would only talk about it in person. I arranged a meeting."

"When?"

"Saturday night."

"Fast work."

"You want me to slow down, Bim?"

I smiled at that remark. "Quinney, huh? There ain't nothing in Quinney."

"We're gonna meet him at a bar in Stockbridge."

"Is the Irishman coming?"

"Does he have to?"

"Yep."

"Then the Irishman is coming."

"Let's go inside. I'm getting cold."

My mind was troubled later that night; not when I went to bed, but at that time in the early hours when I woke up to find my demons down at the end of the bed having a good time with my imagination. When I was younger the demons had to do with money mostly and sometimes a relationship. Those younger troubles couldn't hold a candle to this crew of rascals who liked to torment me now. I am not afraid to die, especially since I survived the strokes and then outlived my wife. I now saw death as a way out of my wheelchair and back into Pat's company. What I feared the most was this life that was ending. I was doomed to die a normal, everyday, and forgettable man. I would be remembered for a week or two and then I would merely become that guy who used to hang out in the garage.

As I lay awake with my mind racing around blind corners I got a fresh jolt of fear about meeting this guy about my bird question. Somehow it didn't seem so bad to drag the family into my crazy whims, but now we were inviting the public. The fact that he was an Indian didn't help much, except, like most white people, I figured they were superstitious by nature and more tolerant of their elders getting elderly. Still he was a stranger and I almost felt like backing out of the meeting. It would be easy enough to tell Sony and Des to forget the whole thing. Maybe I would even go to Cedar Wherever early and get out of the way. I could watch the caged birds and pet the docile dogs and wait for the final stroke. My handicap keeps me from walking, but it does not impede my ability to toss and turn all night in my bed.

Predictably, in the morning I was crabby. Carrie picked up on it early and parked me in the garage to grumble alone. Mike ducked out, too, with just a polite wave before driving off somewhere. I felt awful. I felt like a burden. Worst of all, I felt stupid about feeling anything. I can write about these moods, but I cannot truly describe what it is like to be the garbage waiting at the curb. Maybe I just did.

Around noon Carrie came out with a hot ham sandwich and a can of beer: mood drugs. It was Friday and they were going out to Yeleneck's supper club in the Holyland for fish fry. I was already making up an excuse not to go along when she threw me a curve.

"Melanie was wondering if you would spend the night with Roland. She, Ray, Molly, and Owen are going to a dinner theater in Ft. Atkinson to see a show and spend the night down there. You up for it?"

"Well, maybe, but am I babysitting Roland or is he babysitting me?"

Carrie smiled and nodded. "You both are looking after each other."

I could see no objections. "Funny, I only stayed out there one other time and that's when I got drunk on a Christmas night and big Roland put me in the cheese shed."

"Well, as a matter of fact you will be in the cheese shed again tonight. No stairs there and there is a bathroom. Roland is looking forward to it, Bim."

"I'll bet he is."

Well, actually he was. In fact having me sleep over was some sort of big deal for Roland. I think he liked having an adult around who was unable to walk or drive away. An only child is basically a lonely child. I was one myself and so was the other Roland Heinz. I was envious of my friends with large families, but then I was envious of a lot of things when I was a kid. At least little Roland has this beautiful property to roam around and he is surrounded by interesting people. But, then one of the things little Roland's Papa and I bonded over was our emptiness. Until right now I had always thought of us as good friends, but perhaps we were more like brothers. And Roland did have that adoption thing going for him. I liked the idea of being an adopted brother. Mostly, I loved being out there with the kid.

CHAPTER SIX

Spring is the time to get your motorcycle out and run her if you are a bike enthusiast. I never was, although, I liked engines of all kinds and their mechanics. My preference always was to have a roof over my head when motoring and some solid steel walls surrounding me. Bikers would sneer at that comment, but at least us car guys didn't have to wear Halloween pirate costumes just to go for a ride. I knew a lot of these people and pretty much understood where they were coming from. They were mainly coming from the movies. Films like the "Wild Ones" and "Easy Rider" struck a rebel chord in a way that made it easy to be a rebel. You just got on a bike and presto, rebellion against society. That was okay until it became a pretty non-exclusive club. If you could afford a Harley-Davidson, a leather jacket, and grew some facial hair you were in. It became difficult to be a rebel within a rebellion so over the years these folks tended to all look the same to me. We did seem to share a love of beer, which was some common ground, but like I said, I was a car guy. I wanted my date next to me, not going through my pockets from behind.

Earlier in the evening Roland and I had a nice meal of left-over cold chicken and German potato salad. Instead of watching TV we sat outside and looked at the stars for a while. He knew a lot more about that stuff than I did and he was tour guiding me around the night sky. I have to say I really enjoyed this. Few people bond over the cosmos. After pointing out a sky road called the ecliptic he paused for a moment and sighed deeply.

"What do you think is going on up there, Mr. Stouf…I mean Bim."

"I'm not sure what you mean."

"Well, the universe and all that goes on forever so there must be something going on up there besides, well just some twinkling."

Having spent most of my time pondering the nature of the garage I didn't have much to add to this discussion so I let him expound. "What do you think, Roland?"

"Well, that's just it, isn't it? We don't have anything like a space ship that can go exploring that far out so I guess we can only think about it."

"So it seems."

"But, Grandma Molly says that is what our imagination is for. You turn your brain into a space ship and go and make all that space into anything you want it to be."

"Sounds like you've thought this through," I said, my neck getting a bit stiff from looking up.

"That's what I'm writing my book about. I told you I was a writer like Papa Roland."

Smiling in the dark now, I said, "Your Papa would be proud. What is your book about, son?"

"I am writing about how we humans finally figure out how to do the traveling part and we go off exploring in space."

"Yeah, sounds neat. What are we going to find out there?"

"We find God."

It took me a few seconds for that bit of plot to sink in. Here was an eight year old kid writing a book about some future search party taking a rocket ship to Heaven. I started to say something maybe two or three times, but the words got stuck in my throat. I had always figured that death was the rocket ship to that destination, but this little kid had thought beyond that.

"I think I am going to want to read that book, Roland."

"Cool, I'll bring you a copy someday."

"I hope you're a fast writer."

I kind of wish I hadn't said that. Mortality leaks out of me these days like air from a tire with a nail in it. He just looked at me and nodded his head. There were about ten chapters of his story in that nod alone. All I could think was that I wish I had a kid like that to leave behind. We finished the night with milk and cookies in the cheese shed and he took his sleeping bag over to the day bed. I felt very peaceful as I slid from my chair onto the hide-away. The moon had come up over the Ledge and eternal light was flowing all around us earthlings. Then 'they' arrived.

Somewhere in the night I felt the weight of a person sitting down on the edge of my bed. I assumed it was the boy.
"Roland?"
A voice from across the room answered.
"Yes, it is him, but not the one you think it is."
My eyes shot open and I saw the silhouette of a figure at the end of my bed. It was backlight by a soft blue light. Behind this figure was another one sitting at Molly's writing desk. That figure was backlit pale yellow and was quite large. I guess I should have been terrified, but my reaction was more like stuptified delight.
"What's going on?"
"You're getting a little Ghost Farm hospitality."
"Hello, Rollie."
"Sorry to wake you, Bim, but we both need some help."
"We do?"
The other voice answered me.
"Sometimes we all need help."
"Hello, Garnet."
"Thank you for remembering me, Mr. Stouffer."
"You are unforgettable, girl. How are things in the cosmos?"
"Just fine, I suppose, but we are in the cheese shed in Pipe-a."
Whether I was dreaming or being haunted I was going along for the ride. Before I could think of something clever to say the blue figure got up off the bed and went out the door into the yard.
"He wants you to follow him, Mr. Stouffer."
I guess you do what a ghost tells you to do so I followed Roland out to the yard. He was bent over and picking up pieces of paper from the grass just as I had seen him doing in my other dream.

"What's with the litter clean up, Rollie? Is that what you do now that…"

Roland's color flamed red and he spun around and glared at me as if angry. I could feel my heartbeat speed up and started to think about finding a way to wake up.

"Yeah Bim, I'm the fucking cosmic garbage man. What do you think about that?"

"Geez, you really are mad at me. Why, Roland?"

He paused and his color returned to cool blue.

"Because you are just standing there and not helping me."

Nice dream trick, I thought. I am actually standing and walking. I then bent down and picked up the pieces of litter, but then realized they were not pieces of paper, but small white feathers.

"Feathers?"

"*Yeah, feathers, Bim, as in flight. When was the last time you tried to fly?"*

"Roland, you know I can't walk let alone fly."

"*Bim Stouffer, take a little walk around your imagination!"*

I woke up lying in the grass outside the shed just as the sun was coming up. My face resting on a carpet of violets and little Roland was nudging my shoulder.

"Wake up, Bim," he said. "Are you okay? What are you doing out here in the yard?"

There were a lot of things flying around in my head, but I think I had a grip on the circumstances of my nocturnal activities. I rolled onto my side and smiled at the boy.

"Hah, must have done a little sleepwalking. Just bring my walker out here and I can get up, okay?"

I watched the kid go back into the shed as I sniffed the freshness of the morning. I decided to keep my 'visitation' to myself. On the way back inside I noticed that there was nothing to indicate that I had done anything but just simply walk out of the shed in the night. So, old Rollie wanted me to walk before I could fly. Looks like I had taken my first steps. I had my own glow on the rest of the day.

The great bird pow-wow took place in the old saloon in the middle of Stockbridge. This little town was not too familiar to me. If I went north of Fond du Lac it was usually on Hwy 151 and Stockbridge is on Hwy 55, which continues due north when 151 turns east toward Chilton and Manitowoc. I did a little web research and learned that it was named for the Stockbridge Indians, an Oneida (Ho Chunk) tribe that was relocated from New York State because someone at the time thought that was smart. It struck me that sometimes these relocation things worked out for the better for the injured party. Who would not want to be in Wisconsin rather than New York? But then I am white Cheesehead and never had to be put off my land for any reason. It makes me scratch my head sometimes to think how arrogantly history is determined.

Sony and Des were not talking much on the way up so I just shut up, too, and watched the sun set over Lake Winnebago in a rather spectacular fashion. My head was still buzzing from the ghost visit the night before, but I was gradually rationalizing the whole thing as a vivid dream brought on by my own guilt and fears. As for how I had gotten out into the yard, I was in denial. Every time my brain brought it up, I quickly thought of something else. Like crazy red sunsets.

Lionel Littleman was about 65 I'd guess. He looked like some Indian I remembered from a Paul Newman movie, but I think that guy was an Apache. Lionel was a friendly and talkative man, who liked his beer a lot, which made us cut from the same bolt of cloth, I suppose. I got my one and he got his six. Sony and Des ordered wine, which was a brave move in a twist-off top place like that. We also ordered a pizza since they were half price tonight. Pizza and beer, the Eucharist of the Church of Wisconsin. Anyway, here we were. Having assembled my cast of pissed-off lovers and a tipsy relocated Indian I was ready to dive into that which was mostly unknown and bordering the Twilight Zone. And everywhere there were birds, I mused although the only ones I could see were stuffed and mounted with the fish over the bar.

CHAPTER SEVEN

They call the eastern shore of Lake Winnebago the 'quiet side' of the lake, which is a wonderful understatement. The western shoreline is dominated by US Hwy 41 which is what used to be the main road from Canada to Florida across the middle of the country. Rt.41 has lost traffic to the interstates in most areas, but not the Fox Valley of Wisconsin. This road carries Flatlanders to and from their North Woods cottages in the summer. In the fall it mainlines Packer fans from the population centers of Milwaukee and Madison to the hallowed grounds of Lambeau Field. In the winter it is the gateway to winter sports, and in the spring, well the road crews begin to rip it up. I mostly avoided going up that side of the lake, but my wife, Pat liked to shop at the mall in Appleton so up I went about every other weekend. That side of the lake was built by the paper industry and when I was a kid we always held our noses as we passed through Neenah, Menasha, and Appleton. Oshkosh was okay because they made furniture and overalls, which didn't stink. The placid eastern shore is still mostly farm land sloping down from the Holyland and spilling over the Ledge to Lake Winnebago. The east is Roland Heinz Country, quiet, handsome, and slow to change…except for the wind turbines, of course. But, folks are getting used to them and the low hum of a blade in the wind is preferable to a loud blast from a Peterbilt air horn.

"I have a little farm on a piece of lowland just east of here, a bog surrounded by a grove of mature hardwoods. It is a natural bird sanctuary and so I became interested in birds because I live among so many kinds of them," Lionel began. "I have over sixty feeders on my property for song birds, but I also have herons, cranes, hawks, and eagles come over from the big lake. One day a few years back, just before the first snow, I was filling the feeders and I began asking myself the same question that you are now asking."

"Where are their corpses?" I whispered and he nodded.

"Yes, how and where do all these birds die? It is not like I didn't find one or two from time to time. My neighbor's barn cats are prolific hunters and when they kill they usually just leave the body to rot. This is natural around here. Natural, but too rare to account for what we are asking."

"So many birds and so few observations of what happens to them when they die," Desmond said, restating our premise again for his own clarity, I suspect.

"What's your theory, Mr. Littleman?" asked Sonia.

Lionel took a long draught of beer and wiped his mouth with his sleeve.

"It is not so much a theory, as you say. A theory sounds too scientific."

This guy thinks like me.

"What I am going to tell you is something that was passed down to me by my grandfather. He lived to be one hundred and ten years old and knew many things. He only died last year. Maybe you read about him in the local paper?"

Sony and Des shook their heads, but I read the local paper daily and I sort of remembered.

"Littleman," I said. "Yes, I remember that story now," I said. "Hundred and ten year old Indian, I mean Native American, died in Calumetville, right?"

"Right, good memory," said Lionel, "and don't worry about being politically correct about the Indian thing. Nobody I know cares what you call us except other White people." He turned and looked at Sonia. "Do you care if you are called Black, Negro, or whatever?"

"Well, no, but for the record I am from Black and Arab blood. It's just that my generation doesn't care too much about that stuff," she said.

Lionel smiled and nodded.

"Well, I'm fooking Black Irish," said Des, "but we're getting a tad off subject."

He said this with a smile and tapped his finger on the table next to his wine glass and continued. "I want to know what your grand da said before he died in Calumetville."

Have I mentioned I love Des, too?

"My grandfather was a Ho-Chunk shaman. A spiritual man like maybe your priest. Birds were important to our tribe for many reasons and they are often depicted in our art. In this very bar when he was one hundred and six years old I asked him that exact question about where the birds go to die. He told me quite directly that they have a place where they fly to when they feel death is near."

"A place?" I said, "an actual destination?" I felt a tingle of excitement. In truth, I didn't care if it was a fact or a legend. I just wanted an answer for a change.

"Yes, a place. But, this is not a Ho-Chunk story, Bim Stouffer. My grandfather heard it from another person from another tribe."

I heard an 'oh-oh' coming from inside my head. It looked like we were getting at least third hand information, which is borderline fairy tale. I was bound to hear the rest of this, but I now had very serious doubts that this notion of mine would survive the night.

Lionel continued as the pizza arrived creating no distraction.

"In 1968 my grandfather drove over to Minnesota to sit in on the first meeting of the American Indian Movement. He was not a radical, but he was a social activist in our tribe and he was interested in new ideas."

Now I was afraid that Lionel was going to get political. That would not endear him to me. I hate politics more than the Chicago Bears. I folded my arms and listened carefully to where he was going. I noticed Sonia was now very interested and Desmond was, too, because they are both radicals in their own literary and political ways. I think most poets are.

"In 1973, AIM had its famous standoff at Wounded Knee in South Dakota and once again Grandfather was there for support and to learn things. It was at this standoff that he met a Lakota woman, who spoke of a secret place in the Black Hills where the birds went to die."

Now I was interested again. We were back on track. "Do you know where this place is, Lionel?" I asked.

"I am not sure anyone knows exactly where this place is, however it was supposed to be a cave."

"How much legend, how much truth?" Sonia asked.

"Maybe fifty-fifty," Lionel admitted.

I didn't mind those odds. "Okay," I said in summation. "We have a what, bird cave somewhere in the Black Hills? Do you think anyone else has more information?"

Lionel Littleman stretched his arms and then ran his fingers through his long, gray hair. He blew a puff of air from his lips and closed his eyes.

"You want to go and find this place, right Bim?"

"Maybe…well, yes."

"Why?"

I thought that sounded strange and negative. I started to answer him, but my brain was busy doing some calculations. I needed to get to the core of the last hard question of my life. I finally found my voice.

"Lionel, at some point at that standoff in Wounded Knew your grandfather must have been interested in this bird thing or he would not have come back with this story. Why was he interested? Well, I can tell you. In 1973 he would have been about my age. He could not have known at the time that he had all those years left. The dead bird conundrum is triggered by older people who see the end of their road and simply want to know where they are going. I want to know because it's a *meta* something…what is it again, Sonia?"

She and Des spoke at the same time: "Metaphor."

"Yeah, a metaphor. You know that word, Lionel?"

"Sort of like something poetic that represents something else."

"You're smarter than I am, friend," I said. "Look at me. I am old, crippled, stupid, and heading for an old folk's home in a few weeks. Everything will be neatly wrapped up as far as my life goes: dead wives, dead friends, dead ends. The only thing I need to pack is some hope. I am not any walk-on-water religious man, but like my little friend, Roland says, there's something going on up there."

I pointed up and all eyes followed my index finger to the ceiling of the bar and the heavens far beyond it.

"Bottom line, everyone, if the birds gather at some launching pad to eternity, then I figure it will be okay for me to do it, too. I trust their innocence. I trust the poetic metaphor that they left me as a clue. And maybe I could just accept that right here tonight and go home to bed, but that ain't how Bim Stouffer lays things to rest. If there is a bird cave in South Dakota I wanna see it!"

I must have said the last part kind of loud because a few guys at the bar turned around and smiled at me. I couldn't think of anything else to say or do so I took a slice of pizza and began to eat. I avoided eye contact with my tablemates, mostly for effect.

"Well, I guess that settles it," said Desmond O'Conner in that matter-of-fact tone he has perfected.

"Settles what?" said Sonia Costello in her everything-Des-says-is-BS tone that she owns.

Then my friend, Des, summoning all his Irish charm and wisdom utters the words that lights the fuse that brightens up the night.

"I think it's time to be taking a wee bit of a road trip," says he.

Well, I thanked Lionel for his information and got what little extra details he had about this possible contact in South Dakota. I had a name and a place to start. While he and I talked Sony and Des had their own pow-wow in the rear of the bar away from my ears, I suppose. It didn't matter what they decided because my mind was made up. I had my quest, or at least the outline of it: go to South Dakota and try to find the bird cave. If it was there I was determined to see it. If it was merely a legend I was determined to learn the legend. If everything else failed I would at least get to see Wall Drug before I died. The ride home was interesting.

"Do you know how hard a trip like that would be on you, Bim?" Sonia asked me for maybe the third time.

"Hard? What's hard is just sitting around waiting to leave my house." I knew this would bruise Sony a bit, but she was badgering me so I had to badger back. It is what Wisconsin badgers do.

"I get that, Bim," she said, "but you have to consider everything before you follow some whim."

"Well, isn't that a good word: whim!" I snorted. "I brought you two into this because it *was* a whim and you two are the only people I know on this earth who would take a fucking whim seriously."

Silence.

I hear Des clearing his throat in the back seat. The poor guy is now trapped into taking sides. I know he likes whims, but I also know he loves this woman and fears her scorn. Sonia saves him before he can declare himself. And then what again sounded like poetry to me comes out of her mouth.

"Okay, I have nothing, but time for a few weeks. Des?"

"I have nothing, but time as well, love."

"Okay, so let's start talking details instead thinking of excuses not to go," I said.

"The first detail," Sonia observed, "will be Carrie having a fit. She is not going to want you to go on a road trip. And she'll be pretty much right, Bim"

I was starting to get a little angry again, but decided to take a different tack.

"Listen, kids, this is not some big dramatic production, okay? We would be going on a relatively short trip to the Dakota's to have a little fun and get me prepared for the Cedar Asylum. I will pay for everything out of the cash I got for my car and we can probably do the whole thing in a week or ten days tops."

"Let's at least drag it out to two weeks," Des enthused. "If it's to be a proper quest and all."

"That's the spirit!" I said and slipped my hand over the seat back so Des could low five it. "You leave Carrie to me. What's the worst thing that could happen on a short road trip?"

Sonia looked over at me and I expected a laundry list of worst things.

"We could run out of Depends."

Now Des stuck his hand up front to high five her. And with that sign I knew it was all going to work. As we flew past Ghost Farm on the way back into Fond du Lac I thought again of the ghost of Roland Heinz and my nocturnal stroll in his yard. Maybe some pieces of the puzzle were coming together. Maybe a whim, a lark, or flight of fancy had been missing from my life all along. I felt happy and brave. If you, dear reader don't want to know if there really is a bird heaven then now is the time to close this book. I ain't promising you nothing right now except a final answer. What more can you ask?

The imagined battle with Carrie never happened. We all sat down at the kitchen table and everyone came into accord. The trip was on, although I know Carrie and Sonia would have several serious conversations about how to keep me alive so I could die later back in that other place. I got the feeling that Carrie and Mike would have liked to come along, but that would turn it into Bim's Bird-Brain Bus Tour. I wanted to bend this thing back into an up-beat spiritual quest. Jokes were fine as a selling point, but down deep this was no joke. We planned on leaving the day after tomorrow, which would be June first.

I now had maps running through my head at night, which was an improvement over the scary sneak previews from Anxiety Theater. It occurred to me that what goes on at night is much more important when you are say, past sixty. Maybe it is because we lose some energy and staying up late is virtually impossible. Instead of TV talk shows until midnight we have our own programs on the Sandman Network. I paid no attention to dreams as a kid. I never could or cared to remember them. Now I want to analyze every one of them. We have the World Wide Web so why not the cosmic internet? They say brain function is all electric and chemical so what's the difference between my computer screen and my dream screen? I guess I had better stop asking such hard questions of myself before bed. They are the equivalent of eating a Braunschweiger sandwich with raw onion and a kosher dill before sleep. Sweet dreams, all.

CHAPTER EIGHT

In yet another one of my useless ponderings I was trying to figure out what day, month, or year it was when I evolved from a wise-cracking curmudgeon into this rather polite senior citizen. Don't get me wrong, my first impulse is still to be cynical and critical of everyone and everything, but the words don't come out of my mouth like they used to. I think the first pieces of the old me left when the first stroke came. I read somewhere that people who had major heart surgery woke up and never felt like their old selves again. It seemed possible that a whack to the brain could have the same result. When Pat died I felt like I have been encased in plastic shrink wrap. I was preserved with a perpetual, benign smile on my face because I was embarrassed to ever show anger again. Things like this make me wonder why mankind has never been able to build a time machine. Maybe if desire was the mother of invention we could take vacations back into our pasts and see who we used to be. Lately, I have this overwhelming urge to put a cigarette behind my right ear and lay a little rubber on Main Street. It makes me smile to think of that so maybe I did travel back in time for a bright second.

The first weekend in June around here is usually Walleye Weekend or better known locally as Tattoo and Spandex Fest. Okay, that's pretty cynical. Bottom line is I would rather be hitting the road than patrolling Lakeside Park with half of my walleye sandwich's butter and sauce on the front of my shirt. That's happened every year since I have been in the chair. In truth, it is a nice way to see friends and neighbors that you don't see otherwise during the course of the year. Besides them, I do like to see the rustics come into town to stare up at the tall buildings of the Fondy skyline. I actually used to compete in the walleye fishing contest back in the day, but I never caught much when it counted. Winnebago is still a good walleye lake and you combine that with Mercury Marine having their home offices here and you get a nice festival. I hope everyone has fun, but I will be elsewhere.

Once the die had been cast for hitting the road everything went smoothly. No one made a big deal out me leaving the safety of the garage for the Wild West and that is the way I wanted it to be. Now, I know there were lots of conversations going on behind my back, but I didn't care a whit about those. I was getting my way and that was all that was important to me. I knew no one was turning back when I was asked by Melanie if it was okay if Roland came along. She said he wanted to go and she thought it would be good for him. So it would be the four of us.

I had a couple days to look at maps and do some research of my own. I calculated the odds of finding this bird cave at about a million to one. Again my kind of odds. I did take Carrie's suggestion and rented a van with a lift gate for my chair. We all knew that there would be frequent stops and this feature would certainly make things easier for everyone. It turned out to be no more expensive than a regular van so why not? The van came the day before we left so we could practice. Instead of riding shotgun for the trip I decided that my spot would be in a captain's chair with a drop down table in front of it. Perfect for writing and near the gate. It was also within easy reach of the mini-fridge for my daily beer.

I had never been what they call 'well-traveled.' My folks never took vacations beyond driving over to the Dells for a weekend or going down to the Zoo in Milwaukee once in a while. I know they worked hard just to get by and did their escaping through television, which is how a lot of people 'traveled.' Speaking of TV, I have not watched the thing in years except for glancing at the occasional Packer game. Come to think of it I might have moved to the garage as a reaction to television. The damned thing was always on in the other house and my first wife was a total addict to it. She wasn't the only one.

I remember when those big screen TV's became popular. Actually all they had to do in this town is sell the first one. No neighbor could stand walking past the house next door at night and seeing that wall of animated color without having to have their own. Then there was that hi-def thing, whatever that is. My eyes are so bad, who the heck cares if the picture is crystal clear if it can't get past a cataract for cry-eye? Besides all the technical stuff, it was the same old crap night after night. In my not so humble opinion, TV died when Carson retired. End of story. End of TV rant.

The roll out for the trip was a little anti-climactic: we merely left. We decided that Sonia would do most of the driving since Des still had that Euro-tendency to wander over into the left lane. It was my choice to take the back roads whenever possible because I wanted to purposely slow down the trip and I wanted to see the scenery go by at a viewable speed. Interstates are for people in a hurry. It is too much like flying low to drive at 70 mph, anyway. If you want to get someplace fast go to an airport.

Des rides shot gun and Roland is back here with me. Everyone has been quiet as we drove out of town and into the countryside west of Fond du Lac. I attribute this to the uncertainty of the objective of the trip and the flat out beauty of the farm country in June. Upon entering Ripon, Des breaks the silence.

"Look there, Sony, the birthplace of the Republican Party."

He is looking at a neat and well-preserved little white house in the middle of town. I should have known it would be something political that would get the conversation going.

"Those were a different breed of Republicans back then, Des," says Sonia. "The parties sort of switched ideology somewhere along the way. Lincoln was a Republican and he freed the slaves. Do you think that party would do that today?"

"I never could understand American politics. They seem so mean spirited and rigid."

I didn't want to jump in, but Des is my straight man. "Not like Ireland where if you don't like the other party you just lob a bomb at them, eh?"

"It's not like that anymore, Bim."

"My dad says politics is a team sport and people root for the one they grew up with no matter how it affects them now," Roland offered.

I was going to want to turn around if this went any further. I should have kept my own mouth shut. I saw Sonia preparing her lecture and had to stop it.

"Please, everyone, no more!"

I guess I made my point because silence took over the trip again. This was not going well and I wondered what I could do to set the correct tone. I wanted to stress the spiritual part of my road trip and quest, but all I could think of were stupid road games like billboard alphabet or 'I see something.' I noticed Roland had his lap top open and was on line.

"How'd you get on line out here, Roland?"

"I have a hot spot modem. It works anywhere a cell phone works."

"No kidding?"

"You can hook on, Bim, if you want."

"Anything interesting?"

Roland tapped a couple keys and then turned the notebook toward me so I could see the screen. "I found a place called Eagle Cave here in Wisconsin."

"Let me see that," I said and he handed me the laptop.

It turned out besides the name, this cave had nothing to do with birds and seemed to be just another roadside tourist trap out west of Madison. I was not sure what I imagined my bird cave to look like, but this sure wasn't it. They even had their own brand of cheese.

Sony, who had been listening asked, "Anything, Bim?"

"Naw, lots of pictures of Cub Scouts with cave helmets on. Besides, it's too far off course."

"What exactly is our course, Bimster?' asked Des.

"Sony has my map. We mostly take the back roads across southern Minnesota and South Dakota. And anything you see that you want to stop and look at we'll just stop. All of you. I want lots of pictures, postcards, and souvenirs for my jail cell at the Cedar place."

As we meandered through western Wisconsin I got sleepy— peaceful sleepy. I closed my eyes and listened to Sony and Des chat as though they were a talk show on the radio. I liked it that their tone was friendly and even intimate. Maybe there was hope for those two. Little Roland had his chin on his chest and was snoring softly. The late morning sun was coming in on my side of the van and making my closed eyelids glow a warm red. I drifted away.

We stopped for lunch near the Dells and it was one of those antlers-on-the wall places that kids love. And if kids love a place you had better learn to do the same. This place had a gift shop, too, full of the usual junk: knick-knacks, cute little cans of maple syrup (from some other state), Indian crafts, and lots of Wisconsin jokey things like foam cheese hats, and every mutation of Bucky Badger. I hate to admit I love browsing those stores and Des pushed me around patiently while we waited for our table.

I ended up buying a ceramic pine tree that caught my eye. Des wondered why I chose it and I told him I would tell him later. Lunch was traditional road food: the special was chicken pot pies, which everyone ordered. They were delicious and even from my wheelchair I was able to snatch the check just ahead of Sony's reach. It was my trip for cry-eye and I realized that there would never be a check at the place I would end up. Besides, I had a wad of money and a Visa Card burning a hole in my pocket. Besides that, I still like to feel like a big shot.

On the road again with full tummies the atmosphere in the van was much cheerier than it had been in the morning. There was a lot of tacking to do to drift slightly north toward Viroqua and eventually Minnesota, but Sony had the GPS programmed and it was fun jumping from one obscure road to the next. At one point Des leaned over the seat.

"Okay Bim, why the pine tree?"

The Irishman was not only a storyteller, but a good listener and gleaner of tales.

Sonia asked, "What pine tree?"

"Uncle Bim bought a souvenir tree at the restaurant," Roland informed her and I had my audience primed and ready. It seems I also had a new nephew!

"This is a story about your Papa," I began. I saw Sonia's eyes light up in the rear-view mirror, Roland closed his computer, and I already had Des smiling at me directly.

"Me and your Papa were rolling home one night down Park Avenue…the one in Fondy, not New York City. It was early December and you know how the houses are all lit up for Christmas like they are competing with each other, which I guess they are. There was a fresh snow early in the day, but the night sky had cleared. We had been dropped off after work at the fish bar up by the park so we had to walk the mile or so back down to our neighborhood. You could say we were enjoying each other's company on a cold, clear night with the proper amount of antifreeze in the veins."

"Careful, Bim," warned Sony with little Roland in mind, I assume.

"It's okay, Aunt Sonia, I know it means they were drinking. Keep going," urged Roland. I obeyed.

"Well, besides trying not to slip on the icy sidewalk we were doing some philosophizing as men in our condition were apt to do. And as such we came around to the life and death things that always come up."

"Careful, Bim." Sonia again.

"No, I get it. I want to hear this," said Roland the Lesser.

"I asked your Papa what he thought happened to us after we, you know, pass away. He stopped walking and exhaled a few puffs of frosty breath into the vast night. He then pointed up to the top of a beautiful pine tree in the yard of a grand house. He said Bim, look at the very top of that tree. Look at the point at the top. What do you see? I looked up and saw just at the very top point of the branches a very bright star. It was like the tree was an arrow aimed at the light. I see a tree and a star, Rollie.

"He said he figured that the tree was rooted to the ground and the star was floating way out there somewhere. He said that dying was to climb the tree and follow the arrow to the star. He said he figured it would be quite a trip from there. Lots of handshakes, hugs, and kisses with missed loved ones and friends along the way. He said it would be a lovely walk just like tonight with no pain ever again. He gave me an elbow in the ribs then and we both laughed and moved on. Well, I thought I had just heard the truth as if from God himself. I admired that man that much. Believed everything he told me. Now I see a pine tree and it always reminds me of my friend, Roland and that wonderful moment."

"That's neat, Bim," whispered Des O'Conner.

Sonia smiled again with a glance in the mirror. I took the little ceramic tree out of the bag and handed it to young Roland Heinz Hitowsky. His expression was priceless, but I am not a good enough wordsmith to describe it more than that.

CHAPTER NINE

I suppose it was economics that made the wayside go to the wayside. As we drove along I noticed that most of these pull-overs were closed or at least the restroom facilities has been closed down or removed. What a shame. My family didn't travel much except in Wisconsin to see relatives and the wayside was always a must stop. Most of them had those historical markers as I recall and my dad always made a history lesson out of them. I think the local American Legion Auxiliaries or some ladies club would maintain a rose garden and keep the place neat. Folks often picnicked there even in the days before the restrooms and bubblers were added. Us kids always peed in the bushes anyway, but what the hey. When the johns came so did the vandals and there was more of an excuse to loiter. See how that goes? You keep fixing things up until you wreck them. Now a country road crew mows the weeds twice a year, but every once in a while a rose sticks it's head out of the prairie grass like a boutonniere worn on the lapel of the past.

We stopped early in Viroqua at one of those charming roadside motels that has one story and you drive right up to your door. I only describe this detail because there are not many of these places left. Everything these days is some sort of 'Suite.' Anyway, I think we had spent enough time confined to the van for the day. Also, I am in charge, right? Viroqua is a pretty little Wisconsin town that didn't seem to know that the 60's had ended long ago. I love that. It is just enough off the beaten path that much of the ugliness called progress can't find the place. I think I had some cousins here at one time, but then again it might have been Verona. Long gone cousins and towns that begin with a 'V' confuse me. Definitely time to stop and rest.

I had been thinking all day about how we were going to do the roommate thing. It seemed logical to me that Sonia and Des would shack up in one room and Roland and I would share the other. I did, however, suspect it would be more complicated than that. I was right. Sonia was definitely not being lovey-dovey enough with Des to let her nephew get a glimpse of unmarried adults sleeping together. I already knew Roland well enough that he could care less and was more of an unmarried adult than he was a kid. In the end we got a cot for Roland and all the men stayed in one room while Sonia had a room to herself. It was simpler that way. For the time being.

We got Subway sandwiches for dinner and held a quest meeting in my room. I half expected Roland to be more interested in the cable TV than talk of bird caves, but he was truly a member of the team. Geez, he was even taking notes!

"According to Littleman, the woman's name was Lorelei, but we have no last name." I stated just to get things rolling.

"A Lakota woman with a German first name should be good enough," said Des. "but if this woman is still alive she would have to be what?"

"Nineties or older," Sonia guessed.

"Well, Pine Ridge is not that big and I am guessing there are records. We should be able to find a relative or someone who might remember her," I said.

Sonia's phone went off, but she just looked at it without answering. "It seems to me a bit of folklore like this cave would be general knowledge. Why would it be a secret? Honestly, I know next to nothing about Native American customs, but most people like to talk about their heritage. They're proud of it usually."

I rummaged through the sandwiches looking for my tuna sub. "Unless they don't want outsiders snooping around sacred places. The Black Hills are still sacred to the Lakota even though it has been turned into a tourist trap with Rushmore and all that crap. I might hang on to anything that is not already exploited if I was them. Of course, I hope we can find someone to trust us. We're from Wisconsin which may be enough to get us scalped."

"You'd better get those stereotypical ideas out of your system here, Bim," Sony warned and I instantly knew she was right.

"You're right, of course. Let's make a pact of respect right now for not only what we are looking for, but the culture that surrounds it. The cave may not exist, but the people do."

"Well said, Bimster," said Des. "You can't kiss the Blarney Stone without kissing a lot of Irish lips."

Sony rolled her eyes as Roland tried to parse the analogy. Me? I know Des' BS when I hear it and love it. We broke up as evening began to darken into a starry night. Sony went to her room to return whatever phone calls she had piled up and Roland indeed wanted to watch some tube. Des asked me if I would like to go out for a push and I gladly accepted. There was a bumpy sidewalk heading toward downtown under large leafy trees. I felt relaxed and content with our first day on the road.

"I always wanted to ask you, Bim how you and Pat hooked up. Story?"

"You want a story or a road map, O'Conner?"

He had to think about that, but not for long.

"Ah, you mean Ms. Sonia and me self?"

"Seems to me something's gotta give someday. It's been quite a few years of dancing for you two."

"Let me think about that while you tell me about how Pat Stirling became Pat Stouffer."

I noticed fireflies blinking on and off above the lawns, although we called them lightning bugs when I was a kid. The soft yellow lights easily brought Pat to the front of my mind.

"Well, after my wife Helen died the first person to ring my door bell was Pat Stirling. She lived two doors down and we had always been friendly, but Helen's personality never allowed anyone in the neighborhood to get too cozy. Especially a widow. Anyway, she came in with a dish to pass of scalloped potatoes and ham and after she set it down she gave me a simple grieving hug. I realized it had been years since a woman had hugged me in my own house. Des, I think I heard bells.

"That hug led to a bowling date and then some supper clubbing for the lonely hearts. I found myself looking for excuses to walk down to her house just to bum a cup of coffee. I have to also admit that I really liked her garage much better than mine. One Friday night we drove out to Yelanek's for fish fry and we got a little tipsy waiting for our table as usual. I leaned over and kissed her right at the bar, which was a huge statement on my part. You know me; I am rather buttoned down emotionally. Anyway, when we got back to her place we watched Carson and actually necked on the couch. And you know what, Des? It's more fun the older you get."

For just a moment I lost my place. The chair seemed to disappear from under me and the lightning bugs blended with the stars. Remembering love is so sweet it makes your teeth hurt. I knew I could pull Patsy back in from the forever whenever I wanted, but I savored those moments as though they were numbered. I felt the strength to stand up and walk right then, but I let it blow out of me in a long sigh.

"So you two fell in love just like that?" said Des, breaking the spell that probably needed to be broken before I started bawling.

"Yeah, boy, just like that…and then came the trip to Vegas."

This part of the story at least held some comic relief.

"Spin me around and I'll finish the story on the way back to the motel."

Funny what a 180 turn can do to an evening.

"It started out as a church junket for cry-eye. Some sign-up sheet that someone posted in the rec hall. I guess there is no better place to find travelers to Sin City than the church. Well, we thought it would be fun to actually take a trip together and Las Vegas was as good a destination in February as any. Neither one of us had ever been there and it would be fun going with friends. The party atmosphere on the plane was revealing. Church stiffs that you would never think capable of stand-up comedy were wearing lampshades before we left the ground. And don't look at me like that, Des."

"Like what?" He was behind me in the dark, but I knew how he was looking at me.

"I thought about acting up, too, but I didn't. I just held on to Pat's hand."

"Wait a minute. You had never been on a plane before!"

"First time. That doesn't matter. I behaved. Let me finish, okay?"

"Proceed, Bimster."

"We land and there's a couple buses waiting to take us to the hotel. We were at Caesar's Palace, which I thought was cool, but it was already sort of passé because of all the new amusement park type hotels on the strip. It really doesn't matter once you're inside because they are all the same past the front door. Flashing lights, money sounds, and the occasional shrieking winner. I know Pat felt a little funny about getting one room because of the church angle, but we did and spent very little time there anyway.

"We were frugal and meek gamblers at first playing quarter slots and walking around. Pat liked the people watching more than the gaming. Now as you know I like to play and on day two I had enough guts to sit down at a blackjack table. With Pat's hand on my shoulder I hit a hot streak against a dealer who kept busting. I quickly racked up about fourteen hundred bucks. With the luck and the comped drinks I was feeling like Sinatra when I cashed in at the cage. I had never had that much cash in my pocket. We went to a piano bar off the lobby and drank some more. I remember Pat telling the bartender how to make a Wisconsin Old Fashioned. I don't think they pour much brandy in Nevada.

"So there we are feeling no pain and it's just past noon or something. I want to go to the room, but I see a flicker in her eyes so we go for a walk down this shopping arcade. A fateful walk it was, Irishman. We stop at a kiosk for the Wishing Well Wedding

Chapel and stand the proper distance so the sales gal doesn't know if we are truly interested or just curious. Well, she knows. Next thing I know I am reading a brochure about how easy it is to get hitched in Vegas. They have various packages depending on how much you want to spend. Well, I got money, a woman who seems interested, and a buzz on.

"Next thing I know we are in a limo heading for the courthouse to get a license. Sixty bucks, no waiting. They laugh at the Wisconsin ID's and make Cheesehead jokes. Back into the limo to the chapel. I pay $900, which provides us with our justice of the peace, a witness, some flowers, and some pictures just in case we don't remember. More cheesehead jokes and Mr. and Mrs. Stouffer are back in the limo to Caesar's. It is now about two in the afternoon…on Valentine's Day. The rest, Mr. O'Conner, is history."

We had just gotten back to the motel where Sonia and Roland were sitting at a picnic table in the courtyard waiting for us. Funny, after telling that story I felt like a bridegroom again. Nice feeling, but I was dog tired and ready for bed. Roland came in with me leaving Sony and Des alone for a while. The kid helped me get ready for bed, which touched me deeply. He is such a good kid. I hope I don't snore too much for him.

CHAPTER TEN

So this is America. Like I said, I never traveled much so places outside of my tight circle are more like vague concepts or dots on a map. You know they are there, but they only exist in the mind like flying numbered balls in a bingo machine. Driving from town to town in another state is a wonderful dose of reality. Concepts become places, places become people. I am still a simple man, but the road does turn us all into philosophers. There is a hard-to-explain delight in just reading the menu of some coffee shop that you never knew existed, but then it has its regulars who never knew you existed. The subtle differences between Upper Midwesterners separated by only a few hundred miles make you wonder about coffee shops in Timbuktu or Outer Mongolia or somewhere on Mars. You see, I can tell that my days are numbered because my mind is like a lost plane looking for a landing strip. Note: I wrote this on a napkin at a little diner in Blue Earth, Minnesota. Their coffee is so strong that it feels like someone is knitting the hairs on the back of my head. I love this trip and somehow this morning everyman is my brother and every woman is my sister. There is a plate on the wall with an inscription in either Norwegian or Swedish. I ask the waitress to translate: Kaffe er den beste av alle jordiske drikker: Coffee is the best of all earthly drinks. It is today!

Detours deflected us off my route and forced us to cross the Mississippi near LaCrosse. Well, its spring in Wisconsin so they gotta fix the roads while they can. My complaint is that every time I saw a sign proclaiming "Men Working" I saw no one working at all. There were people there, but they were always standing around discussing something or another. Probably where to have lunch or what bar to go to after 'work.' As you can tell I am cranky again today and I need to get rid of that feeling. I do notice that Roland is amused when I get this way. With his placid parents he has probably never been exposed to a crotchety, old garage sitter before and no doubt thinks I am some sort of living, breathing Muppet. One good thing, Sony and Des are holding hands sometimes up front. As we cross into Minnesota I think of something that I have always wondered about.

"Hey, Sony."

"What's up, Bim?"

"Do you remember that the cougar that attacked Owen originated in the Black Hills?"

"I was pretty young when that happened, but yeah, I knew it came from somewhere far away and into Wisconsin."

"They ran the DNA and traced it," I said, "but my question is how did it cross these big rivers to get into America's Dairyland? I doubt it walked across one of these bridges."

"Do they swim?" Des wondered.

"Do you?" I snarked and Roland giggled.

"I swim like an eel," said Des.

"No comment," said Sonia.

"I don't think cats swim much and look at that current down there. Mark Spitz couldn't swim across that," said I.

"Who's that?" said Roland.

"Some old Olympic dude with a mustache," said Sonia clearing the whole thing up. Sort of.

"Well, that cat didn't fly so how did it get across?" I thought it was going to be a mystery, but not much stumps the kid.

"Well, Uncle Bim, what if it waited for winter and walked across on the ice. If the weather was cold enough even a big river can freeze in places."

The three adults all stared at the little guy and smiled.

"Bingo!" said Sonia.

"By George, I think he's got it," said Desmond O'Conner trying to affect an English accent.

"Yeah, Roland, good thinking," I said. "One mystery solved. On to the next."

The border region between Minnesota and Iowa makes Illinois look like Switzerland for cry-eye. We found a frontage road that they call 'the old road' that paralleled the interstate and stuck to it. Actually, this wasn't bad: no trucks and plenty of roadside amenities at the crossroad exits. The only problem was navigating around slow farm implements and locals in no hurry. I noticed a breed of driver who sort of reminded me of mobile garage sitters. These were older men, presumably farmers, who drove real slow so they could check out what was going on with their neighbors. I imagined that they were checking to see if anyone had a new tractor or what kind of seed (those planted hybrid signs) was going in that year. It was the opposite of me sitting in the garage watching the world go past me, but I got it.

Sonia was very patient with all of them. I think everyone was enjoying the sunshine and the motion so much that we had reached the point where the trip was the thing. No one wanted it to go by fast or end. This is the magic of travel. We'd gone off to look for America, as Simon and Garfunkel had sung back in the day when I was singing along with them on my car radio. The bird cave seemed to have been pushed to the back burner by the sheer delight of clicking off grain elevators one by one as they came and went on the horizon.

Just before we got to South Dakota we spotted another one of those old motels and delighted the owners by getting our two rooms. I took a nap before dinner while Des and Roland went for a walk in beautiful downtown Luverne, Minnesota. This was another charming main street town tucked away in the heartland. Pipestone buildings and big, leafy trees. I told Roland to take his camera and capture the place. He liked the assignment.

I woke up when Sonia gently rapped on the door.

"Come in, it's open."

She peeked in backlit by the afternoon sun.

"You awake?"

"Yeah, what's up, Sony?"

"I wrote you something, Bim"

Ah, well, that had me wide awake and curious. Sonia Costello is and always will be a poet of note. Sometimes we took her talent for granted because we knew her so well, but having a Costello poem written for you is like Picasso handing you a free sketch. She sat on the edge of my bed as I switched on a light. I read this:

WHERE
There are so many of them:
Billions of tiny heart-powered wings
From the lawns and trees, and wires
And the skies of our lonely planet;
Into the nights and days of our time.
And if their magical aero-waltz
Is not enough to ponder enviously
I have a question about their other mystery.
I know, like us, they are mortally frail and
I know they can fly when angels fail, but
Where do they fall to when they expire?
They seem to disappear without a sound
Somewhere between ether and ground
Does an unseen hand rescue their souls
Somewhere on the way down?

The bird cave was back on the front burner.

Crossing into South Dakota was nothing different geographically speaking, but it was the state where my quest would end so it made me think several different thoughts as we crossed the invisible border. I considered how gradually the trip had become more important than the objective. Let's face it, the objective was a unicorn, the road trip was fun and real. It also brought me closer to the pivot point: the place when I would turn around and face the rest of my life. Standing between me and that point, it seemed, was Wall Drug and some place called Reptile Gardens.

Roadside tourist attractions have always been part of the road experience in this country. I remember the one time we actually took an out-of-state trip one summer when I was a kid that was dominated by black and white "See Rock City" signs heading south. And then when we headed west there was some place named "Pete's Café" somewhere in Missouri that had invested an awful lot in advertising. We never saw Rock City, but I seem to remember Pete's Café. It was nothing special, but I guess it paid to advertise. Wall Drug I suppose is another ad-heavy junk shop, but why the heck is there a Reptile Gardens in South Dakota? Florida, maybe. Arizona, perhaps. But, Rapid City, South Dakota? I took a little comfort in the fact that there were no "Visit Bird Cave" signs painted on every barn, grain elevator, and billboard.

Inside the van I detected some interesting subtleties between Sonia and Des. It was almost as though they were what we used to call spooning. Apparently, their recent problems had been fixed by their night together. If they were known for running hot and cold they were definitely in hot mode now. I found I really like this sort of lovey-dovey atmosphere. It created a harmony that we were going to need. The landscape had turned bleak: treeless hills and less farm country. Roland was often without his modem connection now, but he never complained. He just picked up his Kindle and read quietly. We spent the third night in Winner, South Dakota, which seemed like the last outpost before true Indian country. It was time for a group meeting again.

"Tomorrow we will be getting deeper into reservation land so I guess we should talk about a few things," I said. I was most concerned about Roland and what he might be seeing. "Roland, it's a fact that there is an alcohol problem among some Native Americans and you might see some strange behavior as we pass through. I don't want you to think that everybody drinks too much, but some do." I plead with my eyes for Sonia to take over.

"Native Americans have never had much tolerance for alcohol," she went on, "and it is a sickness, not just a bad habit. Do you understand, Roland?"

Of course the kid understood. He lived in a state where drinking was a pastime.

"Yes, Aunt Sonia, Mom and I talked about it before we left. But, it seems to me that when we traveled to different places it was the poor people who drank and got sick. Dad said it was because they were without hope and drank to escape."

This from an eight year old. God knows his grandpa and I did a little escaping in our day. In fact, this kind of talk always made me a little uncomfortable because I hate hypocrisy and exploring alcohol abuse tended to turn a lot of people into hypocrites.

Des jumped in. "I think the point is we don't stare at people who are drinking or engage them. They want to be left alone and we are going to be not only strangers, but guests when we are on the reservation. We have our mission to learn about the bird cave and we will need help. Let's ask for it with a smile, okay?"

"Well said, Irish. Okay, that settled, here's the plan. We drive to Wounded Knee and see if anyone remembers this Lorelei woman. If that is a dead end we go back down to Pine Ridge and ask around the tribal offices. If that is a dead end we just take a little tour of the Black Hills and maybe ask some locals what they know. Any other ideas?"

"There might be some old survey records in Rapid City," said Sony. "As long as we are going to come this far we might as well dig as deep as we can. The Black Hills do not cover a huge area and most of it has been prospected and mined. Somebody has to know something."

Yeah, I thought, she's absolutely right. I suddenly felt lucky again. It was all out there ahead of us just waiting for a goofy bunch of Cheeseheads to solve the mystery of the birds. Stories would be told about us. Songs would be sung. Hah, more likely jokes would be told, but it didn't matter.

"What do you guys want for supper tonight?" I asked to change the subject.

"Winner, winner, chicken dinner!" chirped Sony.

Chicken dinner in Winner it was.

After dinner I got Des to help me take a bath. I felt as happy as a splashing baby in that tub that I was sure had seen many an old wreck before I was lowered in. Des, bless his heart, brought my daily beer and set it on the rim of the tub. I have learned to savor moments of pure happiness these days, and I allowed myself to float away for twenty minutes down a slow river to the sea.

CHAPTER ELEVEN

The story of the morality of how Native Americans were treated by European settlers is astonishingly lacking in our history. The way I see it we pushed them off their land, exposed them to white man's diseases, and got them liquored up and made docile along the way. How do you reconcile all these things done to people who were here first? Well, you can't, but then over the course of many years, when the dust settled and we had a sea-to-shining-sea nation we suddenly got interested in Indians again. They became side-kicks to our hero cowboys on TV. They prompted a spiritual awakening by appealing to young people who longed for a simpler world. Black Elk speaks to hippies. We adopted their names and totems and made them our sports icons. We all of a sudden loved and revered these people we almost killed off. I think they did the same thing in Australia with the aborigines. Growing up in Wisconsin I never thought much about being a white guy because there weren't a whole lot of other ethnic people to compare myself to. We always had a few Indians around, but they looked, dressed, and talked like we did. When a few black families moved into town it made some people edgy. There goes the neighborhood and all that crap. I admit to mumbling a few epithets from time to time before I got to know a few black guys at work. Then I read somewhere that Native Americans referred to Negroes as black white men. I got it. End of story.

Day four of our journey began with severe weather warnings. The Weather Channel showed a very bright red line of storms coming right at us so we decided to hunker down at the motel for a few extra hours. We all used the time to make some phone calls. Roland called his mom. Sonia and Des called their agents, I think. I couldn't get Carrie so I decided to call Molly. Owen answered the phone.

"What's up, Bim? Where are you?"

"Someplace called Winner, South Dakota."

"Everything still going okay?"

"We got some bad weather in the area so we are in a holding pattern right now, but yeah, all is well."

"Hey, Molly just walked in. Hold on."

I heard Owen introduce me in the background and then Molly came on the line like audible sunshine.

"Getting homesick, Bimster?"

"Jah, if I had one. How's Mrs. Perfect this morning?"

"Well she was busy working on a manuscript."

"You working out in that cheese shed then?"

"Yep, as usual."

Then I thought of something I had been wanting to ask her.

"Molly, you ever see any of them ghosts out there?"

She paused for a brief moment.

"What made you ask that, Bim?"

The storm that we were waiting out had just arrived. The wall cloud had turned the morning into midnight and the first lightning bolt that was close and loud knocked out the electricity in the motel. Molly heard it through my cell phone.

"What was that?"

"A storm just arrived in Winner."

"Oh, okay…so you saw a ghost in my cheese shed? When?"

"Well,…oh, forget I mentioned it, okay?"

"Was it Roland or Garnet?"

My turn to pause.

"Both of them, but it might have just been a dream…except…"

"Yeah?"

"Molly, I woke up in the yard. I think I walked out there to see Roland."

"Did that frighten you?"

I had to think about that question.

"No, I liked it."

"Yeah, I know the feeling. We should talk about this when you get back."

"Sounds good."

"Everything else okay? How's Roland the Lesser doing?"

"He's great. Oh, and the other two are acting like they are in love again."

"I figured that was about due to happen again. Keep me posted."

"Will do. Good to hear your voice, Mol."

"And youse, too. Bye for now."

I sat there and felt weird for a minute or so and then as if acting on some cosmic cue, a bird flew into the motel room window startling me. Whether it was due to the storm or just by chance I would never know. I wheeled my chair over to the window and looked down just in time to see it fly away, but a few feathers were left on the side walk. The wind quickly picked them up and blew them away. It was a moment that flashed of omens and the hair on the back of neck stood up and tingled. If the storm had picked up the motel and dropped it in Oz I wouldn't have been too surprised. The air was crackling and so was old Bim.

Since the storm front was to be followed by an all-day rain we decided on a change of plans. Once on the road again we veered off into Nebraska and decided to stay in Chadron, which was a college town with good accommodations. When the skies finally cleared around 3PM we decided to do some sightseeing. That notion took us back across the border into South Dakota and landed us at the Prairie Wind Casino where no small bit of reality was waiting.

Okay, yeah we have Indian gambling casinos in Wisconsin. I understand that the gaming business is about the only industry left to our Native Americans. People like it, it works, and it's profitable. But, to see a glittering casino and hotel amid these starkly beautiful chalk bluffs and rolling hills seems a little perverted to me. Once you pass through the doors and into the casino action you might as well be in Las Vegas or Monte Carlo. There is no prairie wind blowing on the inside. Having said all this and bowing to the local loss of innocence, I am a gambler at heart. That my heart is not buried at Wounded Knee clears the conscience to get a cup full of quarters and give something back to the Oglala Sioux tribe. Or maybe take something away from them. Where whistles and sirens blow and lights flash continually there is no morality. While Sony and Des wonder around, Roland stands behind me and gapes at my coin frenzy. He has never seen anything like this before.

"You should have won that one, Bim."

Naw, you were looking at the wrong line. On this machine it has to be the center line. Unless, of course, I put more coins in each play."

"Oh, so you might as well play the maximum then, huh?"

I looked over my shoulder and saw my young Frankenstein as he made his calculations. The last thing I wanted when we got back was a lecture from Melanie and Ray about corrupting the kid. I kind of figured he was too smart to ever get hooked on a losing proposition, but I knew I had better get him out of there. I didn't see the love birds so I asked Roland to wheel me outside. The afternoon was spectacular. Low clouds were flying across the hills making dark shadows moving at dizzying speeds.

"How do you like these wide open spaces, Roland?"

He spun his vision around in a full circle. "I like this a lot," he said, "but if I lived out here I wouldn't spend my time inside this place."

"What would you do?"

"Explore."

"What would you look for?"

"Well, maybe Crazy Horse."

This answer threw me. How did he know anything about Crazy Horse? Then I remembered how he is on the internet all the time, which is a good place for most people with curiosity. A bad place for others, I should note.

"Crazy Horse, eh?"

"Yeah, did you know he was killed at Ft. Robinson in Crawford, but nobody knows where he is buried? You know about him, right?"

I didn't know much, but I figured I was going to get a lesson from the kid.

"So, you would go looking for where Crazy Horse was buried?"

"Well, not so much look for it, but explore and see what turns up."

Before I could consider how this kid was smarter in eight years than I was in eighty, Sonia and 'Des emerged from the casino. I noticed they were holding hands and wondered what was up, but I already had too much inside information for one afternoon. We headed back to Chadron for pizza and my one daily beer. I referred to it as Happy Minute.

After dinner, I didn't feel well and went to bed early. Something was wrong and I was kind of waiting for something to happen. My heart was racing and I felt dizzy just lying there in bed. My companions were sitting outside watching the stars come out when I sat on the edge of the bed and then vomited into the waste basket. I must have made a loud noise because everyone was in the room immediately.

Sonia drove me to the local clinic where they did some vitals on me and asked a bunch of questions. In this day and age of electronic records the ER nurse had me figured out in less than an hour. My meds needed an adjustment in dosage. Simple stuff that can turn ugly. I actually felt pretty good when we got back to the motel, but Sony suggested we turn around and go back home the next day. Des backed her up. I told them I would sleep on it to get them out of the room. I had no intention of ending this trip on a note like that. It was very plain in my mind that I would finish this quest or die trying. I knew this was reckless and even selfish of me, particularly with Roland along, but we had come too far to turn around. I knew if I did that every day in that nursing home would be filled with what ifs. Regret is no way to end a life.

We had our meeting at breakfast and I prevailed. The fact that I was clear-headed and cheery won the morning. Well, I might have actually had a career as an actor in Hollywood at one time, because I really did not feel that great, but I made a big show of enthusiasm as we headed off to Wounded Knee. Somewhere along the way I forgot how I felt and could feel a little excitement creeping in as we drove up that hill and saw the little church and a small cemetery. There was no one around except for a bunch of loud crows telling anyone who cared that they had visitors.

I don't think any of us expected the reality of this place. It was a place of some historic importance made famous by Dee Brown's book, *Bury My Heart at Wounded Knee*, but it all seemed too peaceful to ever have been the site of a battle, let alone a massacre. There was only a rectangle of ground surrounded by a shabby chain link fence where the mass grave was. Christian crosses and the church let you know that the White Man's religion had taken hold at some point. Des pushed me around the grave and I was struck by how unremarkable it was.

"So this is it?"

"What did you expect, Bim? Des asked. "Tour buses and the Taj Mahal?"

"I'm not sure. Chain link fences and plastic flowers are too…"
I was at a loss for words. Sonia completed my thought.

"Too white?"

"Yeah, I mean there should be at least some feathers blowing in the wind," I said.

"I think it is purposely simple. The solitude and simplicity give it dignity."

"You know there is some profound poetry in all this," Des observed. "I think the fence, the marker, even the fake flowers remind us who massacred who."

Roland had wandered up to the church. He came back and reported that no one was there either.

"Well, with no one around how are we going to make our initial inquiry," I wondered out loud.

"We passed a post office down there," said Sonia nodding her head at a small building down the hill and across the road.

Wounded Knee, South Dakota 57794. Like most small post offices these days it had irregular lobby and window hours. It was scheduled to open at 11AM today and it was around 10AM so we decided to wait. Despite the persistent wind it was a lovely warm June morning. We unpacked the folding chairs and camped out in the parking lot. There was a cell phone connection so Sonia and Roland called home. Des sat with me while the other two wandered off for privacy.

"How come you're not calling anyone, Irish? I thought you had some girlfriend stashed somewhere." I was agitating on purpose and it felt good to be the old me for a minute or two. Des gave me a real dirty look, which I enjoyed.

"Let's not go there on such a fine morning, okay. It has taken me several days to plead my case to Sonia and I won't have you undoing me fine work."

"So what is it, you just bullshitting her or are you two back together? Inquiring minds want to know."

"Yes, well your mind can spin like a weather vane, can't it? Let's focus on your quest for now and I'll update you on me and the girl at a later date."

"I've seen a lot of hand holding and love eyes lately."
"We have feelings for each other, Bim"
"Words!"
"You might be surprised. We…
Des' explanation was preempted by a pickup truck pulling in beside us.

A man got out and walked over and said good morning. He was Lakota from his long black hair to his worn western boots. We were about to meet our first citizen of the reservation. We were also about to meet a little kismet and good luck.

"Top of the morning to you," said Des and why he put on his Irish accent I have no idea, but it was an icebreaker.

"Hey, you're Irish," said the man.

"And you are Sioux," said Des. "Desmond O'Conner is the name and this man is Bim Stouffer of Wisconsin. Sonia and Roland strolled up and were introduced.

"My name is Raymond Bluehorse. What brings you to the rez, if I may ask?"

I took over. "It's a long story, Mr. Bluehorse…"

"Raymond."

"It's a long story, Raymond. Besides seeing the sights and enjoying the weather we are here to find someone. A woman, who used to live around here. You know anyone named Lorelei?"

Raymond Bluehorse obviously knew at least the name because a wry smile came across his face. He took off his straw cowboy hat and ran his hands through his hair. "You're not going to believe this. There is only one Lorelei around here and she happens to be my grandmother, Lorelei Walker. Can I ask what you want to talk to her about?"

My mind was saying 'holy shit', but my lips were talking calm. "So she is still alive, eh?"

"Ninety-eight. Hard of hearing and almost blind, but yeah, she's alive and kicking. But, I can tell you she has not had any strangers asking about her for a long time. Especially, white folk from Wisconsin and Ireland. You'd better explain this to me."

I did the best job I could telling this man why we had come to South Dakota. I told him about Littleman's grandfather meeting his grandmother years ago and what they had talked about. Yeah, I felt a bit foolish, but Raymond was patient and a good listener. When I had finished he blew a little blast of air between his lips and responded.

"I gotta tell you, I never heard of a bird cave. It sounds more like one of those stories the old ones tell. Of course, that doesn't mean it doesn't exist, but if it did it must have reached one of those dead ends that oral histories sometimes do."

"Would it be possible to speak to your grandmother?" Sonia asked.

"How much time do you folks have?" Raymond inquired.

"How much do we need, " I said.

"Well, I will need to speak to her first. She don't like surprise visitors. Her trailer is a few miles north of here and it depends if she is having a good day or a bad day, if you know what I mean."

I knew.

"I got some business to take care of here and then I need to go to Pine Ridge. I can see my grandmother this afternoon. Where are you staying?"

"In Chadron at the Sandhill Motel.
"Why don't you go back and wait for my call. I'll call you one way or the other, okay?

We all agreed that was the best way to proceed and exchanged cell numbers. Roland snapped a few digital pictures and we drove back south out of Wounded Knee and back across the border into Nebraska. From the motel our waiting game began and I was eager for some positive news.

CHAPTER TWELVE

One thing that always catches my eye is the sight of a solitary tree standing alone in the middle of field. I figure there is always a story behind why the landowner decided to let that tree stand while I'm sure many others were cut down and the stumps dragged away. Roland liked them, too. Whenever we passed one of those one-tree fields he would point and say, 'that's my tree.' I reckon it would have been easier to remove an obstacle that would require each generation of farmer to maneuver their tractors around for sowing, mowing, and reaping, but the tree (usually an oak) was tolerated. Actually, Roland Heinz argued that more than that, it was revered, even worshiped. He thought the tree was spared to commemorate the forests that had been removed to make the fields. He also thought it was a testament to someone's deep reverence for the beauty of Nature and a marker for the passage of time. After all, he would say, whenever the farmer worked the field at any given time of year, the tree was changing, aging, and living in a cycle that a man could understand. That fact that no man would ever cut it and count its rings lent an eternal peace and comfort above the roar of a John Deere or Ford.

The drive south took us through the Nebraska border town of White Clay, which only seemed to exist as a place for reservation Indians to get drunk. There was a liquor store that looked like a honeycomb surrounded by drunk bees. I glanced at Roland and he was pie-eyed to see this spectacle. I think we all would have liked to pass through here as fast as possible, but there were intoxicated men literally lying in the road. It made me feel ashamed and helpless at the same time to just drive around them. It was a painful glimpse of someone else's hell. We talked about it a little with the kid the rest of the way to Chadron, but I could tell he was still taking it all in.

"So, those men just drink all day? They don't go to work?" Roland asked.

Des understood that to a certain extent it was an Irish curse, too. He took over the explanation.

"Roland, there is a big empty space in the hearts of people who have lost their pride and surrendered to the oblivion of drinking. Men who drink only to become numb are to be pitied, but in this case there is enough blame to go around throughout history. Alcohol can make you happy in small doses and very sad when there is too much. The Irish are a moody people and drinking brings out the sadness and airs it. These Native Americans are committing suicide in a passive way. Do you understand any of this?"

Roland thought it over.

"I guess I won't understand until I am old enough to drink."

"Don't even start!" said Sonia.

"Aunt Sonia, I know kids at school who have started already."

"At eight years old?" She was aghast, but I thought maybe she shouldn't be. I had similar memories from my youth.

"Yeah, they drink their dad's beer when no one is home," Roland continued.

"But, you won't, right?" Sonia again.

Everyone waited for the little savant's reply. He never disappoints.

"I don't want to do anything that makes me lay down in the road."

And that was the end of an uncomfortable conversation.

While we waited for Raymond's call I got one from my doctor back in Fond du Lac. I was a little surprised to see him on my caller ID and almost didn't answer, but I did out of curiosity. The guy didn't make house calls, but he had found me in Nebraska. Dr. Iglesias was a Filipino with an amazingly sunny disposition no matter what sort of bad news he was laying on you and he had given me lots of it over the years. But, I trusted him so I allowed him to interrupt my trip.

"Hey, Doc, how's the weather in Fondy?"

"It's nice here, Bim, and where are you today?" he asked and I could feel his smile over the phone.

"Western Nebraska."

"That would be Chadron, correct?"

Okay, I wasn't too surprised that he knew where I was. The local clinic here would have shared information with my personal physician through their computers, but I still didn't know why he would call me. Then it occurred to me that Sonia had probably talked to Carrie or Molly and everyone was concerned about me.

"Yeah, seems I have a short leash."

There was a moment of silence while he tried to figure out that idiom.

"Bim, you do know you should not be traveling long distances with your medical condition, right?"

"No one ever said that specifically, Doc. Besides, who cares what an old man does with the time he has left?"

"You have lots of time, but you need to use it wisely."

"Is this a lecture? Because if it is, this call is about to end."

"No, no, wait. No lecture, just advice. I know you well enough to know that you don't like advice, but I am still your physician and it is my duty to inform you about your health."

"Go on."

"Your latest incident was probably triggered by too much exertion. When you travel you have to move around a lot, yes? Your heartbeat became irregular and those meds had to be adjusted. No problem…this time. But, one more incident like that might be much more severe with grave consequences. You read me, Bim?"

"If you are trying to scare me, I'm too old to be scared. Dying doesn't scare me anymore, but I will take your advice to heart, Doc. The last thing I want is to ruin this trip for my companions."

"You slow down, then. And see me as soon as you get back. Promise?"

"Promise."

"Okay, and Bim…"

"Yeah?"

"I hope you find your bird cave."

He hung up and left me pondering a grapevine that could stretch hundreds of miles from the bottom of Lake Winnebago to the Nebraska Sandhills.

I got Raymond Bluehorse's call too late that afternoon to do anything that day. We arranged to meet again at the Wounded Knee Post Office in the morning. His grandmother had agreed to a meeting, but she wanted only me to come to her place, which I quickly agreed to do. I think the other three were disappointed, but we were dealing with other people's narrative now and not just our own. At least by her agreeing to see me I got the feeling there was something she wanted to tell me. I could hardly sleep thinking about how the next day was going to play out.

The next day after breakfast we headed back to Wounded Knee. The morning was overcast and gloomy, but everyone's spirits were sunny. Raymond was waiting for us at the post office and he drove the van to his grandmother's so I could use the lift gate. He gave his keys to Sonia. I could tell she was a little concerned about me driving off with a virtual stranger, but I assured her that I had my cell phone in my pocket and would call her if anything weird happened. My biggest concern was what to say to Lorelei Walker. I knew I had to keep the sarcastic and smart-ass Bim hidden away. I kept repeating the word 'respect' in my head.

We wound our way around a couple hills north and west of Wounded Knee and I got a little idea of how people lived out here. There were few permanent structures and lots of mobile homes and trailers spaced out for privacy. Neighbors were not on top of each other like they are in my town. Within a few minutes we pulled up to one of those half-sizers and I saw a woman sitting out front in a wheelchair. Well, at least we had something in common. I also saw the ramps that had been built to get her in and out of the house. The yard was neat and there were flower boxes filled with blue flowers. When the lift gate hit the ground the sun suddenly came out and the world seemed to come to life much like when *The Wizard of Oz* movie went from black and white to color. Raymond pushed me up to his grandmother.

"Grandmother, Híŋhaŋni waste," said Raymond.

I thought, oh no, she doesn't speak English.

"Good morning, grandson. Good morning, Mr. Stouffer," she replied, which put me at ease.

"Pleased to meet you, Mrs. Walker, but please call me Bim."

"An unusual name," she said with a mostly toothless smile, "And you can call me Lorelei." Her voice seemed a little loud, which usually meant folks were hard of hearing. I turned up my own voice volume just a little.

"Well, Ma'am, Lorelei Walker is a bit unusual for an Indian name, isn't it?"

She chuckled at my remark and then explained. "My mother named me Lorelei after a white woman who came here long ago to treat the sick. Walker is short for Red Walker, which used to be Walks in Red. It was easier to just simplify everything. Anyway, I know who I am. Come in side, Bim, I have coffee on the stove."

Lorelei and I wheeled ourselves inside, but for some reason Raymond did not come in. I saw him go by the window a few times so I supposed he had some chores to do for his grandmother.

"Wow that is strong coffee," I said. I thought it sort of just came out wrong, but she laughed at me instead of taking it the wrong way.

"It takes a little extra kick to get my bones moving in the morning. I make it stronger every year."

"I know better than to mention a woman's age, but can you tell me what your secret is? I doubt I'm not going to match your longevity."

"Maybe you should pray you don't. Let me tell you something, Bim, not too many years ago I didn't even want to live this long. Health issues, worries about money, and local politics made life seem bitter and useless. But, I just kept surviving from one day to the next. Then something happened to change my perspective."

"What was that?"

"I had a vision. Lakota are famous for their visions, you know?"

"Not sure what you mean."

"It is like a dream only you see it when you are awake. I saw myself as a girl just beginning my journey through life and giving birth to my first child. At that time I knew about as much as my baby about this world. Now the world has turned many times and I have outlived all eight of my children. I continue to live for them and learn everything I can learn."

I hadn't noticed until then that the trailer was crammed with books. In my nervousness I had only focused on the coffee and Lorelei's face. Every surface was covered with them and they spilled out the door of one of the bedrooms. And everywhere there were books, I thought to myself.

"You read a lot," I understated with a sheepish grin.

"Yes, I teach myself. This is my school house. This is where my vision led me. I am ninety-eight years old with many years to go before I am finished reading."

I saw the pride in her eyes, but then remembered that Raymond said she was nearly blind. I think she sensed this and picked up a book, put on her glasses, and began to read with the book only an inch or so from her face.

"In the winter night, when the bed is warmest and house is quiet, my dreams depart and I open my eyes to a square of moonlight on the bedroom floor. I sit up on the edge of the bed and strain to see the moon, to see its shape, and gauge its age. I stand and find my boots and heavy coat and the dog is ecstatic that apparently we are going out. Outside the kitchen door is the universe: every star is watching me, welcoming me into the night. I know some of their names and they seem they know mine. They whisper to me through the bare, clacking branches of the trees. I walk into the yard over hard snow. I feel a sense of being loved. Who could sleep through such a courtship?"

She closed the book and smiled at me, anticipating my reaction.

"Roland Heinz," I said, "from *A Winter Light*. You know why I am here, don't you?"

"Raymond told me a few things. He told me where you are from and it rang a bell. I treasure Roland Heinz's books. You and Roland are from the same place. You were good friends, correct? Raymond told me you seek knowledge of a place where the birds go to die. And everywhere there are birds, right?"

I could only nod in amazement.

"I might be able to help you, Bim, but what you are looking for may be more spiritual than physical. Do you understand?"

I nodded and then said, "I would appreciate any direction or advice. I don't even know why I want this so badly. I think I am lost."

I don't know where that last part came from. We both let it hang in the air. I nervously reached for my coffee and once again the strength and bitterness made me blink. Lorelei watched me, I would even say studied me as if determining if I was worthy of her knowledge. I was beginning to feel foolish again and thought of just getting up and leaving this silent scrutiny behind. I went as far as scooting my chair back, a move that caused a loud screech from the linoleum floor.

"No, don't go off," she said. "You're not lost. In fact, you are in the exact right place. More coffee, Bim?"

From there I lost track of time. This woman seemed to understand me when even I didn't. We talked quite a bit about

Roland and his books, which made me shine in her eyes because I was his 'side kick' as she put it. I was enjoying being famous by association so much that I had strayed away from my original purpose. Before I could reroute our conversation back to birds my phone buzzed in my pocket. It was Sonia wondering if I was okay. Lorelei sensed I needed some privacy and wheeled herself out onto the porch.

"Sony, hey sorry I forgot the time. Everything is fine. Even better than fine."

"You getting some good info, Bim?"

"Well, not yet, but this woman is amazing."

"Oh yeeaah?"

I heard the smirk and innuendo loud and clear.

"She's ninety-eight, Sonia Costello." I heard giggling. "She was already a young woman when I was born for cry-eye."

"Sorry, Bimster, couldn't resist. When are you coming back here?"

"Well, it's still going to be a while, I think."

"Okay, tell Raymond that we are taking his truck into Pine Ridge to get something to eat. Maybe we can meet there later. There's nothing to do here and both Roland and Desmond are getting hungry and restless."

"I'll tell Raymond. We'll stay in touch, okay?"

"Okay. Over and out."

When Raymond pushed his grandmother back into the trailer I told him his truck was going to be in Pine Ridge. He was fine with that and went back outside leaving Lorelei and me to get down to the nitty gritty, the heart of the matter. It was time to ask the sixty-four thousand dollar question as we oldsters tend to say.

"Lorelei, is there a place where the birds go to die? Is there a bird cave anywhere around here?"

She bought at little time with a sip of coffee. I sensed she was digging deep into something that had happened a very long time ago. Turned out I was right.

"When I was a child I was raised by my grandfather, a man named Singing Hawk. He was a shaman, a holy man. Back in those days life was pretty hard around here. The last battles were still recent memories and we had lost most of them and all of the wars. The Lakota's spirits were very low and he was in great demand to perform ceremonies to help the people. One of his duties was to collect fetishes to be used in these ceremonies. Most of them had to do with feathers and my grandfather was always on the lookout for hawk, eagle, and any other colored feathers. It was just something he did and he had his regular places where he went to find them.

"He would often make the journey to the Black Hills and come back with many bird feathers that the women of the tribe would fashion into ceremonial gear. Then the white men discovered gold in the Black Hills and everything changed. Those hills were sacred to many tribes and the land had been promised to us for 'as long as the river flows and the eagle flies." Gold made those rivers stop flowing and grounded all the eagles. We were cut off from our sacred mountains.

"My grandfather told me about that time that he was cut off from the place where he got most of his feathers. I remember that he was angry, but resigned to this situation and he vowed to find his feathers somewhere else. When I asked him about his place in the Black Hills he told me he had found a cave that was littered with the feathers and bones of many birds. He told me that he believed the birds came to this cave to die. He believed they did this on sacred Lakota land to make a gift of their feathers to the people. He never mentioned it again. This is what I told that Ho Chunk man at the Wounded Knee Incident in 1973. And then he told his grandson. And then his grandson told you. History books tell the rest of our story. I am sure you have read some of them, Bim"

"Reading history books and hearing history from you are two very different things. I may be a white man, but I can assure you I am not looking for this cave to take anything from it. I just want to see it. My reasons are confusing even to me, but it means something."

I rapped twice on the table with my knuckles for emphasis.

"It means something, Lorelei."

She took my hand in her own thin, bony hand.

"I know it does, Bim. And I am going to help you."

CHAPTER THIRTEEN

And everywhere there were birds. It was Roland's tag line. I knew it had to do with Heaven being populated by birds and Hell not having a one, but it ran deeper than that…and that's pretty deep! A simple Google search will reveal that every culture since the dawn of Man has ascribed divinity to birds. Gods, angels, and even demons had bird wings. Flight was the ultimate means of getting around and it was denied to Man. Then in Greek myth this guy Icarus was given a pair of wings by his old man, Daedalus, who had made them out of feathers and wax. He warned the kid not too fly too high, but of course, being a normal red-blooded Greek myth human being, Icarus screwed it all up. He flew too high and his wax wings were melted by the heat of the sun and he fell. I know there is some moral in there about hubris and such, but who could blame the kid?
Just watching birds is an obsession to a lot of people and it is not just so they can make an entry into a bird watcher's life journal. To Roland, and I suspect many people like Lorelei's grandfather, birds are the focus of prayers: Take my thoughts to heaven, fly my mind to God.

Finding the bird cave and getting access to it, according to Lorelei, was going to be way more complicated than I thought. I guess I was being naïve to think that we were going to get directions, drive to it, and walk inside. The secret that Singing Hawk held was something that he would not share with too many people. He shared the story often; it seems, but not the location of the cave. This meant dealing with the tribal authorities in Pine Ridge, which is where Raymond and I were heading after my visit and sentimental departure from Lorelei's house.

"Your grandmother is a treasure," I said to Raymond as we wound through the mostly deserted landscape of the reservation.

"Yes, she is still as sharp as a tack," he replied, "and she shows no sign of slowing down, mentally anyway."

We rode in silence for a few minutes before Raymond spoke again.

"Did she tell you anything about what you are looking for?"

I could tell instinctively that he was a little uneasy with his role in all of this so I just came out and asked him.

"If I found this cave would it bother you? I mean that some old white dude from Wisconsin rolls in here and starts asking questions that could be interpreted as meddling in the affairs of your tribe."

"It's crossed my mind."

"And…?"

"And part of me wants to help you and part of my wants you to find nothing."

He stole a quick look at me and then put his eyes back on the road.

"You do understand that I mean no harm. I am here because of a dream I had. Your grandmother understood that. She also understood that I have never done anything like this in my life. This cave, if it exists, represents some sort of closure to me of what I consider a less than perfect life. I have never done anything, how should I put it, as noble as this. I am a garage sitter back home; here I am a dream seeker."

He nodded and smiled.

"I guess I am what you call a neo-modern Indian. I tend to put all of our past into a box and wrap it up with 21st Century technology and pop culture. I try, but it just doesn't work. If you live out here on the rez you are always going to be living in the past."

"Jethro Tull"

"Yeah, see, even you got the pop culture thing going."

"I laughed, "Jethro Tull was big back in my day. I couldn't even tell you who sings what now. Or who raps what or whatever the heck they do. But, all that aside, Raymond, the only thing between us is a few hundred miles of geography and a few decades of living. I could have been born out here and you could have been born in my hometown."

"But, that isn't how it happened."

"Hey, I'm only trying to get you to walk in my shoes for a minute."

"As you walk in mine?"

"You ever dream about birds?"

"Last night."

"And?"

"I was walking down a road and picking up white feathers."

"We have had the same dream."

"I know."

We didn't talk the rest of the way to Pine Ridge. Everything had already been said.

I felt like I had been away from my companions for days instead of mere hours. We did the vehicle exchange and I tried to pay Raymond for his time and trouble, but of course he refused. I knew he would, but I had to make the gesture. We shook hands like the dream-mates we were and went back to our own lives. I never saw his grandmother, Lorelei Walker again. Gate keepers tend to disappear once the gates have been opened. I figured it would be the same way with Raymond as I watched his truck drive away. As Roland Heinz always said, life is tricky.

I had been given by Lorelei a list of hoops I would have to jump through to even get permission to look for the bird cave. The list included the Tribal Council, The Bureau of Indian Affairs, and the State of South Dakota. Each was going to require a letter of intent, an interview, and probably a lot of red tape and wasted time. We decided to go back to Chadron and talk about our next move. We had been gone a week from Wisconsin and now I was probably the only one among us who wanted to see this through. I admit that I was slowly drowning in doubt, but my heart was desperately trying to take over my mind. I didn't want or need this internal fight and I feared once more for my health. I took my blood pressure daily and it was up.

I need to sleep more than anything else so when we got back I stayed in the motel while the others went out for supper. The weather had turned hot and windy so I listened to the air conditioner hum me to sleep. It was still light outside, but the motel room drapes were thick and the room was almost pitch black. I never heard anyone come in later because I was light years away in a dream.

I woke up and looked at my watch. It was 2:35 AM. My darkness adjusted eyes could make out the form of little Roland in the bed next to me. Des was with Sony again. I was trying to figure out if I had to pee or if I could wait until real morning when I felt someone sit down on the edge of the bed. The mattress sagged and I figure maybe Des was in the room after all. But, then Des never had a soft blue glow surrounding him.

"Hello, Roland, whatcha up to?"

"About six two."

Where's your girlfriend tonight," I asked without speaking.

"She's next door, Bim."

"Who is she a-haunting tonight?"

"She's visiting Sonia, but she's doesn't want to wake the Irishman. She's afraid of him because she thinks he talks funny."

Despite walking the high wire between fear and the warm comfort of my old friend I had to chuckle. "She's afraid of him?"

"We're all afraid of something."

"You got that right, Rollie."

"Enough small talk."

Roland's glow suddenly turned from blue to a light orange and he flickered like the flame of a camp fire.

"You want to go for a walk or stay here?"

"Where would we go?"

"Down to the cross roads, I suppose."

"I think I am already there. I think I'll just stay here tonight. Don't want to upset your namesake over there."

I saw Roland's head turn toward the figure in the other bed.
He's a good kid, eh?"
"The best."
"Okay, then listen to me. We don't have much time. I am here to tell you to stick to your plan. Nobody understands you except you and me. Keep looking for the feathers."
"What feathers? Where."
"Keep looking for the feathers…"

Roland was gone in a pale yellow blur. A second later I heard little Roland talking in his sleep. I wasn't sure if I was awake or asleep myself, but I did hear the kid say something like goodnight to his Papa. When I looked at my watch it was 3:05 and I definitely had to pee. I positioned my walker for the trip to the john. I felt alert and rested. I should have known Roland would show up again. Then it struck me that I had forgotten what he told me. Maybe he didn't tell me anything and it was just a dream. Crap, what in God's green earth did he say? I finished up and found my bed again. When my head hit the pillow I felt the crunch of down. Feathers!

The next morning we had our usual meeting at a local coffee shop. We needed to figure out how to proceed and find a way over or around this new mountain of bureaucratic red tape. It was decided that Sonia and I would drive back to Pine Ridge and begin to collect the forms while Des and Roland stayed in Chadron and took in the sights. I think Des was relieved to escape the endless waiting around and Roland wanted to take more pictures. Sonia and I left right from the restaurant.
"You're quiet this morning Ms. Sonia. Something on that great mind of yours?"
She glanced at me, half-smiled, and nodded.
"There's something I've been wanting to tell you and I keep putting it off."

"Well, sweetheart, now is as good a time as any." Then I had a thought. "You don't want to head back home do you? I mean…"

"No, no it's not that," she cut me off thank goodness. "I need to tell you something that no one else knows about. Not even my family."

"Sounds mysterious."

"Well, it may not be mysterious, but there are a lot of people who would think it was miraculous."

There was a long pause as Sonia drummed nervously on the steering wheel.

"Bim, Des and I are married."

"What? Jesus, Joseph, and Mary! You're shitting me." Well, that explained some of their recent behavior, but posed a few other questions.

"When did this happen?"

"What no congratulations?" She was smiling like a bride now, I noticed.

"Of course, but this has my head spinning."

"Well, we were married in Dublin about three months ago. It was sort of an impulsive thing like most of our dealings with each other. You see, another thing that no one knows, except our lawyers, is that Des and I are in the process of forming our own publishing company. We were advised that this would work better if we were husband and wife."

"So you got married for business reasons? Geez, Sony."

"No, Bim, we got married because we have been in love for many years. The business deal was the missing excuse, I suppose."

"Excuse me for bringing it up, but wasn't there some recent gossip about him and some Italian heiress or something."

"She was French, but well, it was just gossip."

"And you were sure about that? I was reading on line where…"

"Bim, it wasn't true. I know this woman. I even spoke to her at Des' request. She has a guy about three or four years older than Roland that keeps her happy. The bottom line is Des and I are hitched and we plan on telling everyone when we get back home."

"That will be interesting."

"I know."

"Where are you two going to live?"

"In your house, of course. That okay?"

I suddenly got a warm feeling inside thinking about Pat and my house once again being a honeymoon cottage.

"More than okay." I put my hand on her shoulder and we made eye contact in the rearview mirror. "I love you both, Sony. I only wish I could have given you away."

"Oh Bimster, I love you, too. Maybe we can do some sort of private ceremony and you can give me to the Irishman. But, let's find that cave first."

"Follow the feathers."

"Huh?

"I had a dream last night. Roland gave me that message. What was your dream about?"

"How do you know I had a dream?"

"A little bird told me. You dreamed about Garnet Granger, didn't you?"

"Bim, this is too spooky." I noticed she was smiling with dancing brown eyes. Being a Costello and living at Ghost Farm had prepared her well for these strange events.

"I'd say fasten your seat belt for more spooky stuff. This trip is just starting to get interesting.

The next several hours in Pine Ridge were awful. The people we dealt with were very nice and trying to be helpful, but I am not sure anyone understood exactly what I was looking for. The BIA agent was particularly patronizing. He was a white guy who seemed to be an Indian wannabe. He gave me forms and pamphlets about protecting native sites and environmental impact, etc. He estimated it would take at least six months to clear any kind of request and scolded me that I should have done all these things before I drove 'all the way out here.'

The Tribal office was friendly, too, but they didn't have a clue about what I was talking about either. I was given a booklet on Lakota legends and told that when the paperwork arrived from the BIA they would gladly sign off. I was ready to give up before we even called the State of South Dakota, but Sony made me. I was told that the governor would have to sign off on any historic or scientific expeditions and I was somehow transferred to the state film office. They wanted to assign me a location scout for my next movie. That was an interesting conversation:

"Yes, Mr. Stouffer, could I please have the name of your company for the application," asked a sweet-voiced woman named Bonnie.

"Miss, I don't have a company. I…"

"Oh, you're an independent film company. We have a lot of those coming here to South Dakota. But, you must have a working name. How about the title of your film?"

I was exasperated. "The film is called Bird Cave and it stars Sonia Costello, Desmond O'Conner and Roland Heinz."

"Roland Heinz? Now I have heard of him, but isn't he dead?"

"As a door nail, but he comes back as a ghost in the movie."

"Ooh, sounds very interesting. Your permit to film Bird Cave will require a $750 application fee and I will need a copy of your insurance policy. I need both of those things before we can move forward on this project."

"Checks in the mail, Bonnie."

"Good, anything else I can help you with today, Mr. Stouffer."

"Nope, see you at the premier."

"What?"

Red button ends the call. I needed my daily beer.

CHAPTER FOURTEEN

When I was young I often heard older people talk about how fast their lives had gone by. How it all speeded up with old age. Back then it seemed like Time went by too slow for me. I stared at the clock in the classroom at school willing it to move faster, but was only rewarded with that agonizing, incremental flick of the minute hand. When I went to church I fidgeted through droning sermons and counted supplicants in the communion line to pass the time. I spent endless hours in my room, sometimes as punishment and sometimes because I had nothing else to do. I would watch the sun creep across my window moving a splash of light slowly across the floor from rug to wall and then up the wall before darkness came. I felt ageless and trapped by Time. Then somewhere along the line the trend began to change. I never had enough time for anything. I began 'running' through my life like it was some race I needed to win. What, in the end, I won was old age and the warp speed of getting even older. Friends and loved ones flew away behind my pace and disappeared in the distance of the past. Now, here I am trying finally to find the brakes on this thing called life. I suppose I'd best just enjoy the downhill careening because the brakes don't exist. They never did.

Getting that beer required us to drive back to Chadron where we gathered up Des and Roland for a celebratory dinner; not for our quest, which was now on the ropes, but for the secret marriage that had been revealed. I asked Sony if it was okay to tell Roland and she said that would be fine as long as he didn't tell his mom and dad or Molly. She asked him to keep the secret until we got back and he was fine with that, as usual. The kid was unflappable and digested knowledge with intellect beyond his years. I came to think of him as a peer which of course he was.

Just before we headed to a local steakhouse I got to talk to Des for a few minutes alone in the room.

"Des, you never cease to amaze me. Combining a business deal with a marriage is well, pure genius."

"You can save the sarcasm, Bim. We've been talking about getting married since I got divorced."

"That was a long time ago," I sighed, "but, all's well that ends well. I hope you will be happy. I hope you will be happy in my house."

Des gave me a wary look. I know he was wondering how I really was taking all this news.

"It was either live in your house or that wreck of mine on the Ledge. Or we could have lived in Ireland at my place in Limerick, but…"

"But the taxes would have ruined you both. Des, I am happy that you will be living in my house. I was always fine with Sonia buying the place and having you there as her husband is a bonus I never expected. Just come and see me at the old folk's home once in a while, okay?"

We shook hands on it. Oh hell, it was such an anticlimax anyway. Those two had behaved like an old married couple for years. The marriage was settling to me and after a trying day, a night out sounded good.

At dinner I got a couple more surprises. Apparently, some faxes had arrived for Sonia and Des from their lawyer and one of them was an illustration of the logo for their new company. Sonia passed it around the table and I was the last to see it as Des handed it to me. It read: Bird Cave Publications, LTD. The logo depicted a stylized bird flying into the mouth of a cave.

"We decided on the name a week ago," said Sonia. "I think the artist did a good job, don't you, Bim?"

I was touched. More than that, the way things stood it might be the closest I got to any bird cave in this life time. I hoisted my Guinness and took a deep draught of the Irish mud for luck.

The other surprise came in the form of a cell phone call. I had felt the phone vibrate in my pocket, but it was just as dinner was served so I didn't check it out until we were having coffee and dessert. To my utter surprise it was from Raymond Bluehorse. He had left a voice mail: "Bim, it's Raymond. I am guessing you had a rough day dealing with all the chiefs and pencil pushers in Pine Ridge. Give me a call tomorrow and don't give up hope. I picked up a piece of information today that you might want to know about. Call tomorrow, okay. Bye."

I cued the message back up and passed the phone to Sonia. Her eyebrows went up and she re-cued it and passed it to Des, who listened and then cued it up for Roland. This sounds like a ridiculous way to pass the word, but it worked. We were all recharged if only for one more day. I was more or less reconciled to heading back to Fond du Lac in the next day or so, but perhaps there was a reprieve. I would put that thought under my pillow that night. Just before lights out Roland had a question.

"Hey, Bim, what do you think Raymond has to tell you?"

"Well, that's the main question, eh? Maybe he figured out a way to cut through all this nonsense with the various agencies around here. I guess we'll find out in the morning. G'night, Roland."

"But, maybe he knows where the cave is now. Maybe somebody just told him."

"I love your optimism. You never know."

"Never is tomorrow. G'night, Bim.

Amazing kid.

I called Raymond's cell number as soon as I got cleaned up and dressed, but only got his voice mail. Why are things never easy? I decided a watched pot never boils so I got everyone in the van and we drove to Ft. Robinson, which was only a few miles west on Rt.20. Roland and Des wanted to see where Crazy Horse had died. The scenery between Chadron and Crawford, where the fort was located, turned into more of what I pictured a western landscape to be. Chalk bluffs and rocky buttes cut the sky and we saw our first buffalo that morning. Of course, we have a buffalo farm north of Fond du Lac, but you understand when I say it is not the same.

There is a monument at the spot where Crazy Horse was killed. I had read the historical pamphlets and legend had it that the great Oglala chief could not be killed by bullets. Well, here I am standing at the spot where he got fatally stabbed by some soldier with a bayonet. Once again, life is tricky. What I wanted to know was why the heck did he surrender at this fort in the first place. This guy was the Babe Ruth of Lakota warriors. He was a hero in every major battle against both enemy tribes and the US Cavalry. He was at Little Big Horn and contributed to making it Custer's Last Stand. It didn't make any sense to me. Anyway, these were my thoughts as I stood there and read: ON THIS SPOT CRAZY HORSE OGALALLAH CHIEF WAS KILLED SEPT. 5 1877. He was taken away from here and no one knows or no one is saying where he was buried.

Well, it was just another one of those Lakota secrets, I thought. Good luck to anyone trying to find Crazy Horse's grave because there was a mountain of paperwork and BS between them and it. It was then that the idea occurred to me that that was why there were so many hoops to jump through around here. It was the one way the Lakota secrets could remain hidden from stupid, impulsive white guys like me. Bury them under paperwork, and elusive permits. Wear the seekers out. I pulled out my cell phone and tried Raymond again anyway. Still just the voice mail. Something didn't seem right.

We had lunch at the restaurant at the fort and Roland was having a lot of fun taking pictures of all the old army memorabilia. I watched him and sometimes just the little kid in him came out to play. He wasn't always a man in a boy suit. I was happy he was enjoying the trip. I was also happy that Sonia and Des were married and enjoying each other's company out here in the wide open spaces. I guess I was the only one who was feeling down. I kept thinking of turning the van back east with nothing to show for my dreams, ghost visitations, and goofy ideas. I tried Raymond again. Nada.

I must have been too quiet on the way back to the motel because Des finally turned around and asked me about my mood.

"Bim, don't you dare get down on such a fine day. We have only begun to scratch the surface of our quest here. And yes, it's our quest, all four of us. We all have a stake in this, you know."

"But, I'm the one…"

"You're the one are you?" Des snorted. "You may not know it, but Sonia is doing research in the motel room long into the night. Roland works the internet, too, when you're not around."

"And you, Des?"

"I pray to all the saints in Heaven that you find your cave so that you can take that jewel back home and shine it up the rest of your days."

"Christ, Des, can you ever turn off the poetic blarney? A jewel I can shine the rest of me days?" I faked an Irish accent and we all laughed. Well, he knew I needed that so I guess it was mission accomplished.

"Okay, no more moping from me," I went on. "I can't get a hold of Raymond so I go into panic mode and for what? This is all way too crazy. I'll give it one more day and we can head home with no regrets. We'll do the Reptile Gardens and Wall Drug on the way back and never speak of bird caves again."

Everyone sort of mumbled some sound of acceptance. I dialed Raymond yet again. Nada again.

That late afternoon at beer time we were all sitting outside in the motel courtyard enjoying a cool breeze after another hot day when my phone chirped. I looked at the caller ID and it said Raymond was calling. It was about time.

"Raymond! Where have you been? I've been calling all day."

"Mr. Stouffer?" Not Raymond's voice.

"Yes, who is this?"

"Mr. Stouffer, this is a friend of Raymond Bluehorse. My name is Luther."

"What's going on, Luther?"

"Ray gave me his phone and asked me to call you."

"Why? Has something happened to him?"

Long pause. "Raymond is in jail, Mr. Stouffer."

"In jail? What for?"

"Well, to make a long story short, for trying to help you."

I had to think about that.

"Where is he?"

"Pine Ridge."

"I'm on my way."

"Thank you. Goodbye." Click.

All eyes were on me. I could only shrug.

"You heard. He's in jail and his buddy says it's because he was trying to help me. What the heck have I gotten everyone into?"

"Seems the plot just thickened," Sonia offered.

Once again we passed through White Clay and it's collection of sad men and drove north to Pine Ridge. I had tracked Raymond down to the Pine Ridge Jail, which was run by the tribe. They would not give me any other information over the phone, but his bail could be posted now that he had been arraigned. Yikes, my dream was mutating into a nightmare. Thank goodness Sonia had some experience in dealing with these things because I sure didn't. And Des was Irish which meant American law, let alone Indian law, was out of his league. Roland was clicking away on his laptop getting us directions to the jail.

Upon arriving I learned that Raymond's bond was only $250, which I had in my pocket. His charge was burglary, which sounded wrong to me, but I really didn't know the guy, did I? He might have been a Lakota Jesse James for all I knew. The Indian cops brought him out pretty fast once I paid them, which was unexpected since everything else moved so slow. He whispered thanks in my ear and said we should leave quickly so we did. He climbed into our van to begin the explanations.

Since I was on the hook for the bail I asked the first question.

"What did you steal, Raymond? Burglary means breaking into some place. Your friend said you did it for me?"

He simply nodded and waited for me to settle down. I liked Raymond and his grandmother and appreciated their help so why was I so worked up?

"I broke into the Tribal Headquarters building and stole a couple cases of soda pop."

"What the hell?" I said and then to the kid, "Sorry about swearing Roland." He just shrugged his shoulders.

"That is what they think I stole," said Raymond. "What I really took was a map."

That statement took a second or two to sink in for everyone, but the light bulbs began to come on one by one.

"Are you saying what I think you're saying?" Sonia asked the question we were all considering.

Raymond showed a lot of real white teeth. "I think so."

"Please explain," said Desmond.

"Well, here's the deal. Yesterday morning I went to my grandmother's place to bring her some groceries. Over coffee we ended up talking about you, Bim and your vision quest. She asked me if you were following through on the impossible list of things you had to do to learn anything at all about the cave and I told her, yes. I told her you guys had been all over Pine Ridge talking to the authorities and trying to go through the right channels. Grandmother knew it was an impossible task to begin with, but in her mind it was a test to see how serious you were.

"It was then that she told me that she might be able to help you, but it would involve some illegal actions. You see, she worked at the Tribal Office for nearly 40 years. She knew everything that was in that building and where to find it. Now, she had been retired for quite a while so she wasn't sure what was still there, but she told me where to look."

"And you found a map, right?" I said. I was starting to figure this thing out.

"I found the map that was made by my great grandfather. It was right where she said it would be in the archives. The document was in a box that had not been touched since they moved the offices years ago. The problem is that this stuff doesn't get looked at, let alone removed from the office without the approval of the chief. An artifact this old would never, ever be approved for removal by someone like me and especially not for someone like you."

"I understand that," I said.

"Also, this map is maybe 150 years old and I doubt anyone could make sense of it today. Modern roads were not there in the Hills back then and most of the landmarks are gone with time."

"But, your grandmother could read it," said Sonia.

"You're jumping ahead of me. Indians tell stories in our own way." He was smiling when he said that and Sonia just smiled and nodded.

"We had to have a plan so it was decided that I would make it look like I was stealing some soda from the store room. I broke in that evening and made a mess of the soda on the way out. Before I left I photo-copied the map and put it in my shirt. The original never left the office. I knew they would get my truck ID'd by the security camera in the parking lot so I got picked up with the stolen soda in the morning, but not before I gave the copied map to grandmother."

"What kind of soda?" asked Roland. The little kid had surfaced again for a second.

"Diet Pepsi," Raymond answered and Roland nodded as if approving the theft.

"So your grandmother has it now?" asked Des.

"No, Luther has it. He has the map that has been transferred to a modern road map of southwest South Dakota. The Black Hills. I will get it from him and then we can meet up and see if we can find that cave. I have to tell you, Bim, it's still a long shot, but it is really the only shot you have."

"So where and when do we meet?" I asked.

"How about the day after tomorrow? For starters, you are going to need to buy every park permit that you might need. The last thing we want is some park ranger running us off for lack of permits. It's June and the Black Hills are filling up with tourists. The rangers like nothing more than busting folks without permits."

"Okay, we can do that part," I said, "what else?"

"Supplies. Flashlights, some rope. There may be some climbing so good boots."

This is where reality dropped my heart from my chest down to my feet. I had never really considered that this cave might require my ability to walk, let alone climb. I guess in the back of my mind I was picturing those Wisconsin caves that were wheelchair friendly to some extent. The idea that we would find the place and I could not see it was too painful to contemplate. Sonia, of course, saw it in my eyes.

"Bim, if we find it, we'll get you in there somehow."

"Jaysus, Bim, I'll carry you if I have to," Des added.

"Okay, okay, a few minutes ago we had nothing. Now we got maybe something. Let's find the cave first and then worry about me. What time and where, Raymond?

"Let's meet in the Mt. Rushmore parking lot at 9AM Sunday morning."

"We'll be there," I said.

I heard Roland whisper, "Oh boy!"

CHAPTER FIFTEEN

I know I kind of blew past the news of Sonia and Des' marriage a little too fast considering the fact that it was big news. Big news needs to be digested over a few days and now I am ready to expound. I think since Des' divorce was so long in coming that it defined their relationship; almost turned it into a permanent affair and they got used to it. Getting hitched, in my mind, is either a deep commitment or an excuse for a party. The former comes with maturity and the latter usually ends with quick kids and a quick breakup. I have done it both ways and it still bothers me that I had to warm my heart up in the bullpen with the first marriage and then pitch a no hitter with the second. It isn't fair, but it is mostly true. I knew a few couples that got married right out of high school who lasted, but they were the exception rather than the rule. Of course, the O'Conner's let their love ripen until it almost rotted and fell off the tree. They went from love at first sight to damned near being blinded by fame, jealousy, and temptation. But, in the end, love won out. It doesn't always bring or keep people together, but it always wins out. If you are truly honest with yourself, did you ever fall out of love with someone that you deeply loved? I think we can do a good job of lying to ourselves sometimes, but you can't move someone out of your heart once they have come to live there.

I had mixed emotions all day on Saturday and we wandered around Chadron picking up gear for the next day. I saw Des, Sonia, and Roland trying on some hiking boots and damned me if I wasn't consumed with jealousy. After my strokes I never really minded being pushed around because I had accepted that that was the way it was going to be from now on. Now I felt like more than a crippled man. I felt like I was being punished. Oh, I knew that even if I could walk at eighty years old I would be very restricted in what I could do and where I could go, but the last ten days my mind had taken me out of the chair so often into memories of the past that I wanted to stand up if for no other reason than to yell at the clouds.

After lunch Sonia and Des drove up to South Dakota to get the park permits and whatever other stickers we needed to glide through the Black Hills. That left me and the kid sitting in the courtyard under a shady willow tree. Roland was pecking away on his laptop.

"You working on that space ship book, Roland?"

He looked up and smiled. Nice teeth.

"How did you know, Uncle Bim?"

"Well, sir, I do a bit of writing myself and there is a difference between creating on the machine and just surfing it. You had the rhythm of a writer."

"Yeah, I try to get a little done each day, but sometimes it just doesn't come. Aunt Molly says that's the way it goes. I'm in no hurry, anyway. What do you write?"

"Well, I used to write a column for the newspaper, but I have been trying to put a book together lately. And your Aunt is right, the mood comes and goes."

"What's your book about?"

"It's more or less about what we are doing here. I started it when I got the bird cave idea in my head and I more or less wanted to chronicle these past few weeks."

"So, it's like a journal about this trip?"

"Yep."

"So I am a character in your book?"

"You are."

"Cool!"

Spending a couple hours with the kid mellowed me out. My self-pity eventually turned to excitement when Sony and Des came back with all the park permits. They also had some other 'interesting' information.

"We ran into some people from North Fond du Lac," Sony stated.

"North Fondy, eh?" I said, "what were they doing here, looking for a garage sale?"

"Now, Bim, those jokes are so stale they stink," she said. And she was right. Our northern suburb was actually a pretty neat little town. If they ever got rid of the damned freight yard it might even become desirable real estate.

"At least they weren't looking for a bird cave," Des added and I didn't know if that was a dig or another attempt at Irish humor. I let it slide.

"What should we do with the rest of the day?" I wondered out loud. I needed something to distract me from thinking about tomorrow. Roland had a suggestion.

"There a movie theater in town."

"Do you know what's playing," asked Sony.

"Benjamin Hill. It's a baseball story. I hear its really good," said the kid.

"I like baseball," I said.

"Sony said, "Me, too."

Desmond O'Conner just rolled his eyes. He had told me once that baseball baffled him. It looked like he was in for a couple of baffling hours.

I hadn't been in a movie theater in ages and certainly not since I was in a wheelchair. The Eagle theater was one of those classic small town movie houses on the main street that had gotten an exterior facelift somewhere along the line to make it seem modern. The interior took me back to my childhood: nothing fancy, but better than a Cineplex cinderblock bunker. I got parked in the aisle, which didn't bother anyone because we were practically the only ones in the house. I guess the film was okay, but I wasn't really concentrating. You already know where my mind was. When I felt my cell phone vibrate in my pocket I checked and saw it was Carrie. I wheeled myself out to the lobby to return her call.

"Hey, darlin', what's up?"

"Well, Bim, is that really you? I had almost forgotten your voice."

"I know, I know and I'm sorry. I tried to call you once. And you could have called before this, too, girl."

"I just figured you didn't need me checking up on you."

"So now you are?"

"Right. How is everything going?"

"Well, the trip is fine, everyone is fine. We are in Chadron, Nebraska and going to Mount Rushmore tomorrow. Weather has been super mostly."

"So what about the bird thing? The cave? Anything?"

I debated telling her the whole story or telling her nothing. It wasn't like I was trying to hide anything, but I figured that after tomorrow there would either be a story to tell or absolutely zip. I split the difference.

"Well, we may or may not have some news about that tomorrow. A couple of the local Indians are helping us. It's complicated. No matter what, the trip has been worth it."

She was silent for a moment and I assumed she was trying to decipher what I had just said.

"Bim, don't do anything dangerous."

"What happened to good luck?"

Sorry, I just can't picture you negotiating with the local Indians to find one of their secret places."

I glanced around the deserted lobby. "You watch too many movies."

"Yeah, maybe. Just give me a call tomorrow sometime and fill me in, okay?"

"I promise, Carrie."

"I love you, you old coot."

"The coot loves you back. Bye for now."

I got some stale popcorn and went back to the film.

And so it was dream quest eve. Or, as the Lakota called it, vision quest. I knew I had blown something totally out of proportion based on a fleeting thought and a haunted dream, but old fools and drowning men grab any piece of flotsam that comes their way. Here I was between the Pine Ridge country and the desolate Sandhills. A corner of America that few people have even considered as a destination and that, I suppose is its charm. The spaces are so wide open that chalky buttes lit by the sun can be seen from 30 miles away as if they were within a mile. Even my bad eyes could make out details on a far off wind-bent tree against the setting sun. I loved Wisconsin as my home, but I was falling in love with this place like an astronaut admiring a crater of the moon up close. I knew there was no going back long term to the garage, but this corner of the country was a fine parting gift to my old life.

I had looked at the satellite maps of the Mt. Rushmore area and called Raymond to make sure we would be in the same parking lot. The map showed several. Again, he didn't answer his phone and I vowed to make only that one call. I guess what I really wanted was a little hint of what was to come. I knew I wasn't going to sleep much anyway. When Roland turned in I was still sitting in my chair reading maps like they were scripture.

There was a fly in the room that was annoying me as though it was a piece of my brain that had broken out of my head to worry me. I thought about folding the map into a swatter and going on the offensive, but I didn't have the killer instinct or desire tonight. I just desired peace and maybe a short nap. I found both listening to the fly buzz its life away against the window.

I woke up for my midsummer night's pee around 2AM and headed for the john. Normally, this nocturnal journey would be accompanied by a lot of grunts, groans, and mild profanity, but I tried to keep it stealthy for the sleeping boy. When I got back to my bed I got in and realized that it would be even harder now to fall asleep. Even the fly had stopped banging his head against the window. It was quiet and dark. I was comfortable so I decided to use one of my favorite sleep inducing schemes. I relived my marriage to Pat:

When we got back from Las Vegas and news got out that we had taken the plunge, many of her friends, I'm sure, did a lot of eye brow raising and clucking of tongues. Even I knew I was no catch, but I knew in a small town that any kind of gossip was desirable; especially when widows and widowers hook up. You see, we both had histories that had nothing to do with us as a couple. Friends and families had grown up together in bonds that many times went back to grade school or earlier. Now that we were married we had to combine two histories into one and at our ages there was a lot to combine. Anyway, that stuff all sorts out and pretty soon everyone accepts the new guy and the new gal. On our personal level even I was shocked how quickly we settled into our roles.

Pat and I both bowled, but on different week nights. On the night when she had her church circle I played Sheephead over in North Fond du Lac. And yes, I know some people call it Sheepshead, but I don't. On Friday night we went out for fish fry. I grew to hate fish fries, but that's another story. Pat attended mass a couple times a week, but I was good for about every other Sunday for communion. I figured it took me about two weeks to commit enough sins to make it worth the priests while. Don't laugh. How much trouble do you think you can get into sitting in the garage?

And that's the other thing. Pat had no problem with me hanging out there. She told me once that she couldn't even picture me sitting in the house all day. I suspect she preferred to have the house to herself most of the time. She liked to entertain her friends in the kitchen and with me already outside I couldn't eaves drop or bother anyone. Sometimes my sense of humor went over the heads of even the brightest people. Still does. Anyway, Pat and I shared lots of love and we had that rare marital trait, harmony. I remember once Pat was coming home from somewhere and parked in her usual spot next to the house. I called her over.

"Hey, Honey, do you ever resent me taking over the garage? You used to park your car in there before we got married, right?"

"Well, yes, I did, but I'm just fine with you being parked in here now."

"You sure?"

"Bim, as long as you do the snow and ice scraping in the winter I don't mind. I like the fact that I know where you are ninety per cent of the time."

"More like ninety-nine, hon, but those are just the waking hours, eh?"

"Yeah, when you finally come inside you come in like a lion."

"I'm still a newlywed and so are you."

"That's true, but something tells me you weren't getting much when you lived down the street."

"You know damned well I wasn't, but even if I was you would get me going."

"Big talk, husband, you wanna go inside?"

"Patsy, it's still light out."

"Hah! Shoulda known."

"I'll be in later, babe."

"I'll be waiting."

I woke up just ahead the wakeup call at 5AM. The window fly was already awake and Roland was in the bathroom. This was going to a special day one way or another. We checked out of the motel and hit the yellow brick road to The Black Hills.

CHAPTER SIXTEEN

The only radio program that I would have on in the garage (beside some occasional polka music by Syl Groeshel's recording band) was the ballgame. I was a die-hard Milwaukee Braves fan and I wept when they moved to Atlanta and I could not listen to them anymore. In that period of years before the Seattle Pilots became the Milwaukee Brewers I became a Cub fan because I could get their station loud and clear in the garage. They also had an announcer who liked beer as much or more than I did. Personally, I have never had the animosity for Chicago that most folks around here have. My dad's parents were from Chicago and we went down there from time to time when I was a kid. Honestly, it looked just like Milwaukee to me. Most big cities look and smell the same. Anyway, I was a lousy baseball player as a kid, but I still loved the game, the players, the stadium (old County Stadium) and Roland and I went to a few games together over the years just to get out of town for the day. Roland had a different take on baseball than I did. I was awed by the athleticism and spectacle. He, predictably, saw it as an oddity and a metaphor hidden in a bag of peanuts. But, he was the only guy I knew who kept score the whole game, making notes around the edges of the scorecard. I saved one of his cards and found it one day in the garage. I found one of his margin notes to be interesting: The entire stadium is a bull pen and everyone is waiting for the call, especially the two nuns in front of us who are praying for a savior and save. Neither one showed up again.

It is easy to see how The Black Hills were once called a sacred land. Of course, that translates in today's white world as a place to make a buck. Mt. Rushmore was created specifically as a tourist attraction to bring visitors and their money into the state of South Dakota. The gold rush in the late 19th century was pretty much an illegal land grab from the Lakota, but since they couldn't defend the land, it was quickly gone. Carving a Rushmore-like image of Crazy Horse into another mountain was treated as another insult to every Indian I talked to. I found an astonishing fact on line that I think few people know about. In 1980 The Supreme Court of the United States ruled that the Hills were illegally taken from the tribe and an settlement of $106 million was awarded as compensation. The Lakota refused to take the money because all they wanted was their sacred land returned to them. To this day, the money lies in trust gathering interest and now is worth about $760 million.

That kind of money could really do some good on the various reservations, but to their credit, the Lakota do not put a price on the word 'sacred.' Wanna feel a little guilty? To most white people money is sacred and the Lakota are fools. Before anyone makes a judgment they should drive into The Black Hills for the first time on a beautiful Sunday morning in June. *Sacred* maybe far too weak a word to describe what you see.

The Hills are dominated by granite outcroppings surrounded by trees. The place has a real clean feel to it. Roland was snapping pictures on the go because we didn't want to be late for our rendezvous with Raymond Bluehorse. I think Desmond was the most impressed, and I gauged this by his silence. He had never seen America this shined up and brightly packaged. When he did look back at me he just shook his head, obviously awestruck. I have seen pictures of parts of Ireland that would probably have the same effect on me.

I also was noticing the complexity of the landscape. I had no doubts there were caves and other places that were hidden up narrow canyons that we seemed to pass every mile. In truth, it scared me. I sensed once more that I was in way over my head here. Looking at some place like this on a map does it no justice. The Black Hills are not going to give up too many secrets to day trippers from Wisconsin. At least we found Raymond with no trouble even though he had a different vehicle today.

Handshakes and smiles were passed all around beneath the President's heads that you just couldn't take your eyes off.

"Good morning, Raymond," I said as my wheelchair alit between our vehicles. "Where'd you get those wheels?" I was looking at a gray Ford Escape that was mostly primer with a tint of green. No hubs on big wheels with a winch in front and hitch in back.

"I borrowed this for today. Where we are going requires a little off road driving. Not too rugged, but it is better to be prepared. You should toss your gear in the back and I will explain things on the way. It is better not to talk too much around here."

I looked around and indeed, the parking lot was filling up with tourists. It was amusing how everyone got out of their cars and then just stood there staring at the carvings. We did it, too.

"How the heck did they ever do that?" exclaimed the Irishman. "I mean, gad, where do you begin?"

Roland, of course, knew all about it and gave Des a little lesson about Borglum and Son and their amazing battle against not only the mountain, but financing, politics, and opposing sentiment. The place where Mt. Rushmore is today was originally called the Six Grandfathers, according to Roland's research, and it was a place where the Lakota passed on the way to Harney Peak, which was the highest point in the Hills and the most sacred place. Dynamite and hammers took care of all that. But, still it is impressive. We left my wheelchair in the van and packed only my walker due to a lack of room. Sony wanted to tie it to the roof of the SUV, but I told her to forget it. Where was I going to be wheeled once we got off the paved roads out here?

We drove down the road a short way and Raymond pulled over into a gas station. Yeah, there were sacred gas stations out there, too, for cry-eye. Good thing, too, because I already had to pee and everyone needed coffee. When we were all together Raymond handed out copies of his maps to each of us.

"The first map that doesn't make a lot of sense is the one my great grandfather, Singing Hawk either drew or got from someone else. It would have been handed down from one shaman to the next. It was indeed the place where they went to gather feathers so it is logical to assume this cave was a gathering place of many birds. Grandmother could not say for sure that the birds came there to die or just were drawn there for some other reason."

"Maybe they came to molt?" This one came from Roland again. Geez!

"Who knows?" continued Raymond. "Anyway, this place is not that far from here, but the roads wind around so, as you can see on the modern map, we have to go back to US 385 and turn back south. We will be passing the site of the Crazy Horse Memorial on the way."

"As an aside," I said, "how do you feel about that sculpture?"

Raymond sighed and said, "If they had done it first, it might have a different meaning. We see it as an afterthought. Crazy Horse was a man who would have been embarrassed by it. Personally, I don't think much about such things. The Hills were lost long ago."

"Sorry, maybe I should keep my mouth shut," I said.

"No," said Raymond, "Talking is how we come together."

Everyone nodded and then he went back to the map.

"The cave is off of Hwy 297 so we have to cut back north from that junction. It is back off that road along Loues Creek, which was a major trail back when the Lakota roamed the Hills. We leave the road there and when we find this bluff, right here, the cave should be close by. Somewhere up the scree fan."

"It actually isn't that far, then," said Sonia.

"No, but there is a ranger station on the other side of 297 and some buildings right where we go off road. We are bound to be investigated. They will want permits."

"We got the ones you told us to get," Desmond said.

"Good, but I got us something even better," said Raymond with a big grin.

He pulled out an official looking piece of paper and passed it around.

"Grandmother had some stationary with the tribal letter head from when she worked there. We fixed it up to look like a permit for a film company to do some location scouting."

"Cripes, Raymond, this has the signatures of the chief and the governor of South Dakota!" I said. "How in the heck…?"

Raymond was smiling sheepishly. "That is another one of my grandmother's talents."

"Forgery? I love it!" Des exclaimed. "How good are these signatures?"

"Good enough," said Raymond. "Let's go exploring."

We stopped along the side of the road and glanced at Crazy Horse through passed around binoculars. Raymond was right; it looked a little second rate compared to the four presidents, but still an enormous undertaking. I hope they stop carving mountains at some point. Enough already. Any way we needed to keep moving. This was going to be a one-day shot and who knew how much searching would have to be done on 'foot' before it got dark. When we got to the Loues Creek turnoff, sure enough there was a ranger jeep sitting in front of one of the buildings and its driver was shooting the breeze with another man. Murphy's Law! Oh well, it would be a good test of Lorelei's forged document. I was so nervous my stomach was doing flips. Roland looked at me and rolled his eyes.

Raymond was cool. He just pulled up next to the ranger and got out with the 'permit'.

"Good morning," Raymond began the ranger and other guy nodded. "My name is Raymond Bluehorse and I am taking these folks up the creek here a ways."

"Well, Mr. Bluehorse, I am sure you know you can't go back there on National Forest land without special permission and I doubt…"

At that point Raymond handed the ranger the paper and waited while he read it. It was crunch time for our expedition. Probably better now than when we got in there and could get into real trouble.

"Location scouts for a film?" the ranger said while still reading. "How come I never heard about this in advance? We're supposed to know about this kind of thing weeks in advance so we can assign someone to guide you. This is dated yesterday."

"Look, you and I know how it works," said Raymond, "but this just came up. We were lucky the governor was even in the state to sign this thing." He looked back at us and then leaned into the ranger, but I could hear what he said anyway. "You know how it is with these Hollywood people. Everything is rush, rush, do it now."

The ranger looked at us. Sonia was hanging out the passenger side window looking anxious. The ranger stared at her for a moment.

"Say, that lady looks kind of familiar. Is she one of them movie stars?"

Raymond was quick and jumped at the opening.

"That is the writer and director, Sonia Costello. I'm sure you have heard of her. She was in all the news and magazines a while back. Kidnapped in Africa, remember?"

The ranger remembered and smiled. "Oh yeah, I remember. Her old man was some famous writer, right?"

"Well, it was her grandfather, but you're right."

"Shoot, we don't get no celebrities out here too often." He handed the permit back to Raymond along with a business card. "This has my cell phone number on it. If you get lost give me a call. I'd come with you, but I'm alone at the station today and we have a lot of tinhorns flooding into the park this weekend."

"No problem."

"You know where you're going?"

"Yeah, we got maps. We'll be out in a couple hours."

The ranger nodded and walked over to Sonia. "You have a good day, Ms. Costello. Looks like you're in good hands with Mr. Bluehorse. What's the name of your movie so I can look for it?"

Sonia is quick, too. "Cave of the Bird People. Be out next year."

Roland's eyes were a big as pie plates. He hadn't heard this much lying from adults at one time in his entire life. I loved the whole drama…once we were on our way again.

CHAPTER SEVENTEEN

I have had so few momentous occasions in my life that I approach them with a little fear. After all, when your dreams come true they merely become reality. When they are dashed they become bitter obsessions. What I was looking for with this cave was totally different. If I am honest with myself, which I hope I am, I am looking for a physical clue that the link between man and animal is the same as between earth and heaven. If that sounds awkward and strange then think about it for a second. I never got nothing from any preacher or televangelist when they spoke of Heaven because I knew they wanted money for their services. When some bird hopped up my driveway on a beautiful day, cocked his head at me, and flew away I heard its message loud and clear: "I live in heaven every day and so can you." Then Roland's books hammered away at that theory. And not just birds, although they were the obvious messengers. Every aspect of Nature promised rebirth after death. I will take that hope to the bird cave and pray my soul will absorb a reality I can live with before I die with it.

Roland found that his modem was working probably because we were close to the Ranger Station and they would need cell phone service here in the park. He pulled up a satellite image of our destination and it really wasn't too far off the road. The creek, which was mostly dry, wound back through a narrow valley to the north where it split off into two branches. Our destination was the left fork. That fork twisted around a rocky bluff that extended like a finger into the valley. In the crook of that finger was where the cave was supposed to be. I must say it was drop-dead gorgeous and if I was a bird I would have happily folded my wings and died in this paradise. The satellite image also gave you an idea of how this terrain would look from a bird's eye. It was very distinctive and when you pulled the frame back the finger revealed itself as the neck of a flying bird. Well, you maybe had to use your imagination, but everyone saw it and agreed with me.

The off road drive was actually pretty smooth. Others had been this way many times as there were a lot of tire tracks and some trash lying around. When I say trash, I mean mostly beer cans. I could appreciate this place as scenic retreat to enjoy a cold one, but my god people, pick up your empties! Raymond explained that this meadow had been used for feeding cattle. There was a man-made reservoir for trapping creek water. It was obvious that this place was anything but secret, which worried me. How could I have my spiritual experience amid crumpled Bud cans and a watering hole for beeves?

When we got out of the SUV we had a pow wow, no pun intended. I was perched on the drop down seat of my deluxe walker looking at the maps. Sonia was glassing the bluffs looking for a cave. Roland was putting on his new hiking boots, and Des was wondering what the hell he was doing here. Raymond was on the phone with somebody. It was my expedition, but now that we were here I was trapped in the damned walker and looking at a fan of rocks that looked like the leftover of a landslide. I also was searching the sky and trees for bird life. There was none. I was getting that oh-oh feeling again.

Then Raymond got off the phone he joined us.

"I was just on the phone with my grandmother and she wishes us luck. She confirmed that our map points right over there. He indicated the place where that finger (or neck) connected with the rest of the bluff. That was where I had been looking, too.

"Why don't you guys go up there and see what you can find," I said. "I might as well wait here since there is no way I get up that fan." Everyone looked at me with pity, except Raymond.

"We can get you up there, Bim."

"Oh no, we can't," said Sonia. "Even if we carried you, Bim, it's too dangerous just to walk on that scree let alone carry someone."

126

"She's right," Des concurred.

"No, we don't carry him," said Raymond, "we pull him up."

"How are we going to do that?" asked Sonia.

"That walker looks sturdy. We tie Bim to his seat and pull him up the fan. It will be bumpy, but if we take it slow we can get him to the top."

Des again: "Then what?"

"I guess we carry him," said Raymond, who was becoming my new hero.

"But, what if the cave isn't up there?" Roland's turn to be skeptical.

Raymond took off his hat and scratched his head. "According to the best info we have, that is the place, folks. If there is no cave up there then we are not going to find it. That's why I called Grandmother; I needed some assurance, too. She agrees that it is where the map leads. It's up to you people, obviously, but I think Bim should be with us no matter what. This is his quest."

A half hour later, Sonia called my cell phone from the top of the fan. When I answered it the first thing I heard was, "Oh my God! Bim, I think we found it!"

Fifteen minutes later I was on my back riding the walker backwards up the fan. Now this was not a very steep incline so even if the rope broke I wasn't going to slip too far, but it was bumpy and seemed to take forever. Everyone above me, including Roland was on that nylon rope. When I got to the ledge I felt like I had reached the top of the world.

"You old goat," said Sonia as she kissed my forehead. "You're probably going to float down after you see this."

They untied me and got me upright. I was able to use the walker, if awkwardly, to navigate the ledge. Behind a little stand of pine trees was the entrance to a cave. My heart was in my chest as Des led me in. The first things I saw were the feathers. They were everywhere. Most of them were pretty much rotten and discolored, but it was a good start. The cave was more of tunnel because I could see light coming in from the far end. Okay, I thought it was a big bird house, but was it where the birds came to die?

"Anyone go back there yet?" I said pointing to a second room that angled off to the right away from the rear opening.

"We saved that for you," said Raymond.

"You go first, Uncle Bim." The kid looked more excited than I was.

"Okay, Roland, you give me a hand. We'll go in there together. Lewis and Clark, okay?"

I still can't believe what we saw. As we inched toward that room the carpet of feathers began to take on various colors. The first hues were faded, but they got gradually brighter as we moved forward. *Follow the feathers.* I had to duck and bang the walker over some gravel into a quite large room. The floor was littered with what I thought were crushed white rocks, but on closer inspection I could see they were millions of bird bones. Among the bones were thousands of feathers, some red, some blue, and some striped and spotted. Among the bones, Roland was the first to spot a couple of partially decomposed blue jay corpses. Then a woodpecker, then a red-tail hawk. I was speechless for a moment, but then I told Roland to go tell the others to come in here, but to give me a couple minutes alone. He trudged off and I was alone with my metaphor, my dream quest, and my awe-struck happiness.

If I had realized some sort of practical dream when I was young I might have led a different life. I might have had a successful career. I might have had children and grandchildren. I might have put my wife in a fine house in the country. I might have run for an office. I might have wielded power. I might have lived my entire life in a splendor and comfort if only I had realized just one dream. Now at eighty I realized that I had finally followed through and taken a dream and made it reality. It may not have been much of quest, but it had a beginning and now an end. I stood in a walker in this strangely beautiful place and cried as I whispered for Pat and Roland Heinz to join me. Come and see what old Bim found, my best love and my best friend because I will surely come to where you are and see what you see. Dead birds and their bones and feathers: the airport gate to Heaven. Next departure…sooner than later.

I was composed by the time the others joined me. I tried to listen as they all talked at once. I knew that it was not exactly the moon landing, but it was pretty neat as Roland reminded me. He took a lot of pictures, but when he showed me the digital images on the back of his camera they did not capture what my eyes saw. I was seeing with a brighter light and higher color. Then at some point Raymond reminded us that it was getting late and we needed to be back to the SUV before it got too dark. I reluctantly turned my back on this moment and walked out of the cave without looking back. On the outside, swallows were now flitting among the rocks and they were everywhere.

The descent would be a snap; just a reverse of the way I got up there. I was once again tied to the walker seat and set down on my back. This time Des and Raymond lowered me carefully while Sony and Roland walked down around the edge of the fan. I had to use my hands to push off a few rocks that tried to snag me and I was only about twenty feet from the bottom when the walker got hopelessly stuck. The sun was behind the ridge to the west and the air was chilling quickly. Des called my cell phone and told me they would come for me as soon as they could get down. I couldn't see Sony or Roland. There was a weird moment of panic that came over me. Despite the euphoria I had felt a few minutes before I was suddenly angry and scared at the same time.

The sun then sent a blinding flash into my eyes as it slid down and into a gap in the ridge. I closed my eyes and waited for it to set. It was then that the ghosts came.

"You're right, Father, he's stuck!
"I see that, girl. Good thing we were here today.

"Well, if it isn't the dynamic duo. Hello Roland, Garnet."

"Hello, Bim, whatcha doin' lying on this mountain?"

"Waiting for Godot."

"Ah, a literary reference. You been reading again in that garage?"

"I read all your books in there, amigo."

"What's an amigo, Mr. Stouffer?"

"Means friend, Garnet, in the Spanish language."

"You men speak other tongues?"

"Wait a minute you two. I'm stuck here and you two are just going to gab away?"

"What would you have a couple of ghosts from Wisconsin do, Bim?"

"I don't know, something."

"I have a better idea. You do something."

"Like what, Rollie?"

"Like get up and walk that last few feet to the bottom. These folks that came here with you have been carrying you the whole way. They came together and made this whole trip work for you. Give a little something back. Get up and walk down."

"Hell, you know I can't walk."

"Oh? Remember that other time we got together?

"Sort of."

"Do it again!"

I felt the sun go off my face and I could only see purple spots before my eyes. One spot was tall and other was stout. There was a sudden green flash and they were gone with the sun. I am not sure how or what exactly happened next, but I started working on untying the rope that held me to the walker. I rolled out of the chair onto a flat rock. I remember crawling up on all fours and looking down to where the meadow met the fan. Then a cloud of those swallows descended upon me and I could hear the buzz of their tiny wings beating and a subliminal harmonic chord as they breathed as one. The next thing I knew I was lying in the grass at the foot of the fan and Roland and Sonia were standing over me. They looked concerned until I started laughing and I couldn't stop.

CHAPTER EIGHTEEN

I was rummaging through some papers in my briefcase and came across a copy of my living will. I guess it is called that because it will still be living when I'm not. Pat and I had this done some time ago and it is a good idea to get it out of the way before your health turns for the worse because you can't joke about it then. I remember sitting at the dining room table going over this thing and us making our choices for the end. I am not sure how these decisions get made in the first place, but once you sign, notarize, and file, it is impossible to change your mind once you have stopped breathing. My wife chose to have a wake and funeral mass with a casket. I chose to go up in a puff of smoke with no church service or funeral, but I figured a wake would be a good way for my friends to get together and maybe go have a drink in my name afterwards. In other words you make your choices like you are going to attend your own funeral. What would I like to see and do on my special day? Anyway, as long as my urn gets stored next to Patsy's box I will be okay with the process. So, Heaven is a warehouse somewhere? See how this stuff makes you nuts?

As you can imagine, there was a lot of excited chatter on the way back to our van at Rushmore. Basically, it was disbelief told from five different perspectives, five different takes and theories of what we had seen. The truth was I wasn't sure what I had seen. No, not the cave, that was real enough. We had pictures. But, it was the last few minutes before sundown that lingered with me. I could see a flicker of it in Sonia's eyes, too. There is no way I should have been at the bottom of that fan. I explained to her and Roland that I must have panicked, untied myself, and rolled down the scree field. Roland bought it, but it was no sale with Sony. Des and Ray were unaware that anything weird had happened. They merely assumed the other two had somehow gotten me down.

What do I think? Well, I was there so I get the last word if only to myself. The Ghost Farm ghosts had been in on this from the beginning. The place that they come from obviously saw the future and the past and, armed with that knowledge, they came to help. I think Roland made so many messes in his early life that he wants to help his loved ones and friends avoid their own. The fact that he travels with Garnet is understandable. She is his creation, the child he held in his head and heart all those years and pages ago. I sure don't understand all of it, but I know enough not to question absolute goodness when it knocks on the door. I think Sony has her suspicions; she's heard enough stories about the visitations at her mom's house. I decided to bind the revealed secret of the bird cave with the forever hidden secret of my ghost walking.

Soon would come the moment I thought I would dread: the moment of pointing the car away from the cave. Surprisingly, I had a brief feeling of relief and even a twinge of homesickness. I knew it was going to take every mile on the way home to digest all that had happened. It may not have been much on the surface, but deep down inside I had gone through a kind of change. Perhaps it was the long-awaited arc in my life. I suppose I will figure it all out before we get home.

When we got back to the highway that same ranger was sitting there in his jeep. We pulled up next to him.

"I was just about to come in there looking for you. You folks find what you were looking for?"

Raymond did the talking. "Maybe, could be, not really," he said and I think he may have winked or rolled his eyes at the ranger because the man nodded and smiled.

"Well, I guess you film folks are pretty fussy, eh? Well, good luck."

"Thank you," said Sonia, "maybe tomorrow we'll find the spot we're looking for."

The ranger tipped his hat like they always do and we both drove off.

"Maybe tomorrow we'll find the spot we're looking for." It was Mr. O'Conner doing his best Mrs. O'Conner and he got an elbow to the upper arm for his trouble.

"Where are we staying tonight?" asked Roland.

"We have reservations in Rapid City so it's going to be a late arrival. You getting tired kiddo?" said Sony.

"No, just hungry."

We all were hungry and weary, but sometimes there is a good side to those deprivations and a communal mellowness was smoothing out the growling stomachs and tired eyes. When we got to Rushmore and switched cars again, it was hard to say goodbye to Raymond. I waited until everyone else had shaken his hand and thanked him. Roland even got his email address with promises to keep in touch. When it was my turn I pulled him aside.

"I've been wondering since the day we met, what made you pull into the Post Office parking lot that first morning? You must have known that the place wasn't open and I don't remember you dropping anything in the box. Were you just wondering what we were doing there? What?" I said.

"Yes, well that is curious, Bim. I guess you could say I had a strong feeling that someone needed help. I saw the van with the out-of-state plates and a three white guys and one black woman looking a little lost."

"And that was it?"

"Pretty much. Grandmother was out of coffee so I was going to Pine Ridge to get some".

"So you being there was because of your Grandmother?

"In a way, yes."

"Figures. Goodbye and thank you. You were the missing piece. You and Lorelei."

He just smiled and drove off. So did we.

I originally felt that this story should have ended with that last sentence, but the story of my last days on freedom road were not over and we had the many miles home to cover. Besides, writing is not only fun, it is addictive. Writing down thoughts and events has a soothing effect on my mind. I may not be as good at this as either of the Rolands, but no one will probably ever read this anyway, so what the hey.

I got Roland to show me how to email some of the cave pictures to Carrie and Molly and their replies were almost instantaneous. Carrie, being Carrie wondered what photo shop software I had used, then added a smiley face emoticon, and finally congratulations. Molly was thrilled and said she was glad we found it and happy we were on our way home. I kept thinking what a surprise she and Owen had coming when the kid's marriage was announced. Of course, she would be disappointed that there would not be a wedding per se, but the receptions are where the fun is anyway.

Sorry, South Dakota, but we did not stop at your Reptile Gardens. When we got up on Monday morning the last thing anyone wanted to see were snakes, although they did have a bird show and a prairie dog town. It might have been amusing, but when the road calls you home you usually don't like to stop the first day. That said, as an accommodation to young Roland, we did stop at Wall Drug in, where else (?), Wall, S.D.

We broke my no-interstate rule and took I-90 to get out of Rapid City, which made Wall Drug inevitable. Wall was the gateway to the Badlands anyway, so it wasn't out of our proposed way home. The store certainly lived up to its own spectacular hype and it was crowded with folks like us, who mostly just wanted to say they had been there and had the free cup of ice water. I was underwhelmed, Sonia and Des were semi-disgusted, but Roland was having a blast. I think most of his spending money stayed at Wall Drug as he stocked up on gag gifts that all kids love. His prize was a jackalope bobble head that some lucky person was going to get for Christmas.

Leaving that cradle of consumerism and rank capitalism behind, we drove into the stark contrast of the Bad Lands. This can only be described as driving through the landscape of another planet. I never knew this place was even out here. In Wisconsin we thought the Dakotas were barren wastes full of pheasants and Swedes. The Black Hills and the Badlands are places everyone should visit at least once. Wall Drug? Eh.

Of course, a road trip is not a road trip without car trouble at some point. The rental van had an engine belt break at the south end of the Badlands near a little town called Interior. At least it was close to the Ranger Station so we did get some help from them, but the nearest automotive place with parts was in Kadoka back up on the Interstate. Well, at least we were broken down amid incredible scenery. While we waited for assistance Sonia and Roland went on a photo safari, while Des and I had a roadside beer. It was a nice afternoon for a bullshit exchange.

"So, you never told me, how's married life treating you, Des?"

"Much better than the last time around. You should know that, Bim."

"Yeah, it's like you need practice."

"Well, I for one could have done without the practice. But, to answer your question, I love being married to Sonia. T'is such a true comfort to me after all those years of impossible love and our own stubbornness."

"Well, you had the disadvantage of fame. That brings too many other people into the mix."

"True, but t'was her fame that brought us together."

"And led to your fame."

Des took a long drink and wiped the Guinness foam from his lips. "What a fooked up mess it all was for a time. And now we are both fading stars who are happier now than when we were on magazine covers. Not understanding life itself is what drives poetry and fiction, I'd say."

"And non-fiction is driven by people who claim to understand everything."

"One could make that argument, but let's not. Too fine a day."

My turn to swig and wipe and then out of the blue: "I sure miss Pat. I wish I was starting from the beginning like you kids."

Des nodded. "I wish you were, too, old friend."

We had reached the crossroads of getting maudlin or continuing down the road of a fine day. I steered us clear.

"You had to get 'old' in that sentence, didn't you, Irish?"

"Sorry, man, but seeing you here against the backdrop of these badlands did not exactly bring an image of virile youth into me head."

We both enjoyed a chuckle as the truth is always a checkmate. Sonia and Roland came back with pictures and wildflowers a little before a wrecker pulled up behind us from Kadoka. The belt was replaced, I paid a king's ransom for the service, and we were back on our way into the flat land that would dominate the next two days of driving.

I won't bother to describe the scenery or accommodations on the return trip because they were mostly the same. We stayed at the same motel, passed through the same towns, and often ate at the same diners. The weather in southern Minnesota was blazing on the day we drove through. Getting out of the air-conditioned van for anything was like stepping into a blast furnace. We stopped early not wanting to over-heat the engine as the temperature gauge seemed to go up when the A/C was on full blast. We all took a true hot afternoon's siesta at the motel in Luverne. Later, I woke up and found another poem left on my laptop, but this time it was from Desmond O'Conner:

This is not a wave, no way
Though it shimmers like a lazy ocean
It is flat and hot and fine and
It drips water from my hairline where
Insects work in the shade and then dine

On hot blood, molten red and black
And I'm waiting for the night breeze
Because I know that it will come back cool
Like the subtlest thrill in the trees
And then I wonder how it would feel
To be in a room at any temperature and to
Sit three feet from an oscillating fan and
Just whisper to you softly about this heat
That has nothing to do with waves
Or agitated mercury
Or summertime

     Sounded like the heat had ignited a little passion in the room next door. I know he shared this poem with me because of our conversation in the badlands. He was telling me in his own way how his marriage worked. If vicarious living and poetry are the only tools left to define my lost love life, well, it's better than nothing. And the care it took to place that poem where I could read it surely is the product of a rare friendship. I had learned quite a bit on this trip: history, geography, cultural values included, but learning about my companions, despite close quarters, was illuminating to say the least. None of us had spent this much time together before and we had discovered that we made a great team. I will miss waking up to them all when we get back and go our separate ways.

CHAPTER NINETEEN

I'm eighty years old or as Honest Abe might say, four score. It is a nice round number that will last a few more days before getting ordinary again. The roundness of eighty makes me think of all those life cycles that I have been through and how you can tell you are in one. For instance, a healthy cycle means half-empty med bottles in the bathroom that you check for expiration dates. Unhealthy cycles leave flattened tubes of Preparation H and insurance co-pays. Good financial times will get you a new car, but down times will get you an ulcer or two. Fun times means playoff games at Lambeau. Sad times means your suit coat pocket is filled with those cards they pass out at wakes. Good weather is grilling four times a week, but bad weather means dripping gutters or slippery sidewalks. Every cycle I have been through has been noted, enjoyed, or tolerated from my garage. I may not be the last garage sitter, but I like to think I made the all-star team. Heck, I even slept in the garage a few times during my first marriage. Who among my peers can make that claim? I hope none.

When we crossed the Mississippi back into Wisconsin we all gave a little cheer. We might have just kept going and arrived home late, but no one was really in a hurry, especially me. We stopped in Sparta, a town that claimed to be "The Bicycling Capital of America. To advertise that fact, there is a colorful statue of a man on a high-wheel bike in the park downtown. It was the only person on a bike I saw, but there were several cars around town with bike racks. We found another vintage motel and got ready for our last night on the road. It seemed like every time we stopped moving my mind began traveling back to that cave. I looked at the pictures on my computer and just shook my head. Was any of that real or was it so real that it had moved to another dimension in my mind? I couldn't wait to hold court back home and begin to really craft a legend around that place.

We found a burger and custard place nearby and ate there at a picnic table, which would have been nice except it was dark and the bugs had been drawn in by the lamp over our heads. The result was we ate faster and talked less during this meal. More than the bugs I felt it was a mood brought on by being almost home. Each one of us had images and thoughts stored that needed to be examined. As I was pushed back to the hotel, I proposed a question.

"Each of you, what was your favorite part of the trip? Roland, you go first."

"Well, I liked staying in motels. It's neat to stay someplace and then just drive away."

I hadn't expected that answer, but from a young boy's perspective it made sense.

"I was most impressed with the scenery," said Desmond. "I haven't really seen much of the US and I had never even heard of Black Hills, Sandhills, or Badlands. I thought America was all cities and towns with a Grand Canyon tossed in somewhere."

"I liked the interaction with the Lakota," said Sonia. "Meeting Native Americans on their turf is eye opening to say the least. In a way, they kind of remind me of my people back in Darfur. You know, isolated, poor, but still spiritual. I like that part."

"No need to ask what was your favorite part," said Des.

Before I gave my obvious answer I was struck that no one else had mentioned the bird cave. This gave me a brief moment of doubt about the importance of what we saw there. Was I on some emotional desert island?

"Well, yes the cave was after all my goal even before we left so yeah, that was my high point."

I started to open my mouth to expand on this theme, but I closed it and left whatever was going to come out locked inside. I needed to think about all of this a little more. After all, I had found a cave full of bones, rotten feathers, and guano; not the Pacific Ocean for cry-eye. Later that night I was lying awake and something came to me: it was not so much the physical cave that was important, it was the cave of the mind. It sounded good anyway. Good enough to sleep on.

By late morning we were back in Fond du Lac. I had a lot of mixed feelings as we all hugged and then split up. Carrie invited everyone to stay for lunch, but Des and Sonia wanted to get home and finally let Molly, Owen, Mel, and Ray in on their secret. Roland gave me a big squeeze.

"Thanks for having me along, Uncle Bim. It was a really neat trip."

"You don't know how happy I am you could come along, Roland. It wouldn't have been as much fun without you."

"I'll call you later and let you know what Molly's reaction is," said Sony.

Of course, Carrie overheard this. "What reaction to what?"

Sonia wasn't going to leave her hanging, but she waited until she, Des, and the kid were in their car and backing out. "Des and I got married a few months ago."

"What?" Carrie yelled after them.

"Bim'll explain," Sonia yelled back and they were gone.

I wheeled myself toward the garage, which was open and inviting. "Bring me a cold beer and I'll tell you the whole story," I said. "Mike home? He should hear this, too."

"Mike is in Chicago. I'll be back in a sec." Carried lugged my suitcase and briefcase into the house and then returned a couple minutes later with a cold Pabst for each of us. I got comfortable in my old lawn chair and began the narrative of our journey. I fast-forwarded to the day at the cave, which I figured is what she really wanted to hear anyway. I showed her the pictures and waited for her comments.

"Well, you really did it, didn't you? Mom would be so proud of the way you found the answer to that question. Are you going to write something about it? Maybe an article for the paper or even a bird lover's magazine? I think there would be a lot of interest, Bim"

"I'll have to think about that. I have been writing a little journal along the way, but it is mostly private stuff. Things I would be embarrassed to share. You know."

"Well, write it all down for yourself anyway. Now, what is all this about Sony and Des?"

Well, I thought, in the pecking order of importance the secret marriage of the O'Conner's was probably a little higher on the totem pole than my bird cave saga. I told her what I knew about the nuptials, which was minimal. Or maybe it was my own story was minimal. Either way I was happy to be home and back in my sanctuary. I didn't have much time left to spend there.

Sonia did call me later to fill me in on her mom's reaction to the news. As I suspected, Molly and Owen were very pleased and sister, Melanie was a little cool about the whole thing. Melanie has a history of distrusting Des and over-protecting her little sister. Plans for a reception were already being discussed. While I had Sony on the phone I asked her for Lionel Littleman's phone number up in Quinney. I had decided to give him a call and tell him that his tip had worked out. I thought he might be happy to hear that, so when I got off with her I called him. He didn't answer, but I left him a voice mail to call me back. Why does no one pick up their phones these days? I mean, isn't that the whole idea of a mobile phone: it's always with you? Sheesh!

The next day Lionel called me back and invited me out to his place to visit his bird feeders and talk. Mike was home and volunteered to drive out there. I told him about Littleman's bird sanctuary and he brought some camera gear with him. It was another glorious June day, but there were severe storm warnings for later in the afternoon. I don't know why, but I liked those yin-yang weather days when the sky started out one way and ended up another. Anyway, it turned out Lionel's place was just up and over the ledge from Quinney a ways. The house and barn were a bit run down, but the acreage had a combination of farm land, marsh, and a nice grove of hardwood trees. We passed several bird feeders just coming up his drive to the house, where Lionel was waiting with a morning beer in his hand.

"Welcome to the rez," Lionel shouted. We all shook hands and I introduced him to Mike Gabler once I was parked in my chair.

"Yes, yes, Mike Gabler, the famous photographer. I have a couple of your books. Would you men like some coffee or…" He held up his beer.

The idea of a beer on this fine morning was appealing, but I declined both offers, as did Mike.

"Why don't you show Mike around a little and we can talk in a bit. I'd like to just enjoy the sunshine and the birds for a while. Don't get around too well in this thing, as you can tell."

"No, we can push you, Bim," said Lionel. I keep the pathways mowed and they are pretty smooth. Come on, I'll drive."

Mike grabbed his camera bag out of his car and off we went. First we took a lovely path into the trees and Lionel always spotted a particular bird before we did. His trained eye was indeed miraculous. I would see nothing and he would point. I followed his fingers to several species of woodpeckers and creepers. Mike put the zoom on and was really enjoying himself. When we came out on the far side of the grove we angled downhill to a reedy wetland with birdhouses sticking up among the cattails. Here you couldn't help but see dozens of marsh birds from redwing blackbirds to even a Great Blue Heron, who never moved a muscle as we passed.

As we headed back up hill to the farm Lionel pointed out a huge nest high in an oak tree.

"That is the home of my most famous neighbors," he said. "I have a pair of Bald Eagles living there, but they are probably down fishing at the lake this morning. Maybe you can see them later."

At Lionel's kitchen table we all had coffee. I noticed the Ho-chunk brew was not as strong as the Lakota, but still hair-raising.

Mike took his cup with him back outside to look for more photo ops. It gave Lionel and me a chance to talk. I gave him the quick version of our trip ending with the discovery of the bird cave. He listened carefully to my tale and never interrupted. When I finished he rocked back on his chair and smiled.

"So you found it. I would have bet this farm it was all a rumor or some lost legend. It must be very satisfying for you to complete your quest."

"Well, yes and no," I sighed.

"Huh?"

"I learned a couple things about myself the last couple weeks and one of them is maybe that the quest is more important than reaching its goal. Someone once sang in a song, *it's got to be the going, not the getting there that's good."*

"You mean there was a letdown. I understand that. It's only natural. But, at least it was not a lifetime quest. You were not on this one that long, right?"

"Not long, but I am starting to figure out it was indeed a lifelong quest. I just didn't know it. I have been looking for answers all my life and this is the only one I ever came close to resolving."

"Well, that's good, eh?"

"Yeah, but there could have been bigger and better questions when I was younger. It took me eighty years to really take aim on something and follow through.

Lionel got up and refilled my coffee mug. I could tell he was thinking.

"So what you are telling me, Bim Stouffer, is that this bird cave was truly the metaphor we talked about before. How does it all fit together?"

Coffee sip. "I thought the cave would answer a question I had about the afterlife. I wondered how flying creatures left the earth for the eternal sky. I found that place, I guess, if only in a very regional sense, but it has gone from miraculous to kind of ordinary in my head since I was there. In other words, I think it was only a small piece of a much larger puzzle."

"I think I see. This has happened to me a few times. That is why they call them mysteries. You had an adventure with your friends and found a puzzle piece. Maybe that is enough?"

"Yes, I believe it is."

On the way home Mike noticed I was quiet and he glanced at me a few times probably trying to read my mood. I decided to lighten it up.

"You ever see any of those ghosts at Ghost Farm when you stayed out there?"

"Well, I heard plenty of stories, but nothing first hand. Why'd you ask?"

"Oh nothing, just was wondering if you could catch them on film if you was to try. I heard people claim they could do that."

"I have photographed many spooks, but they were all living breathing humans. I wouldn't know where to begin with the other kind."

"Me either."

CHAPTER TWENTY

Aging means breaking a lot of old habits from your younger days. Some of them are health related and some get tossed aside just to keep you sane. Even though I was assured that I could still have my one beer a day when I went to the assisted living place, I decided I would leave that habit in the garage on 5th Street. I tried to estimate how many cold ones I had had in that garage, but my beer math is kind of fuzzy. Let's just say there was a lot of aluminum recycled within those walls. I have never allowed myself to think that the beer contributed to my strokes. I preferred to think that it had prevented them from being worse. Towards the end, I felt a little patronized when folks made a big deal of giving me my one harmless beer. After all, drinking one was like drinking none, right? It was all symbolic and I was never much for symbolism. A six pack was just right back in the day. The math was simple and the buzz was perfect. I wondered how I was going to replace a symbolic habit. I figured something would turn up that was more important to me than obsessing over 12 oz. per 24 hrs. And sure enough, it did!

I ducked into the garage as soon as we got back and settled into some more reflective thoughts of the trip. All I could really come up with was that it was over and I had maybe two more weeks of garage sitting before moving out to that home. Carrie and Mike took turns coming out with food as if they understood where I wanted to be all day. As evening crept across the yards and rooftops of Fond du Lac, I finally thought about going inside for the night. I looked at the kitchen window and saw Carrie. It was Carrie, but for just a second it was her mother, my wife, Pat framed by the window and backlit like a holy picture. I had explored a lot of ideas all day, but now there was only one left to act upon. I called Carrie on my mobile and asked her to come outside…and bring a beer.

She handed me my beer and sat down next to me.

"You feeling okay, Bim? You've been acting funny all day since you went out to see that guy. Mike noticed it, too. Did he say something that upset you?"

"No, no, nothing like that."

"Then what? You've got me worried."

"I apologize for being distant, but I needed to think something through and I have come to a decision."

"I'm all ears," Carrie said. I always liked that expression.

"No you're not. You, Carrie Gabler, are all big beautiful blue eyes.

She smiled and blushed a little. I continued.

"How soon could I get into that Cedar Place?"

"What?"

"I'm ready to move. How soon can I do it?"

"Bim, the house sale doesn't close for another two weeks. Are you sure you want to leave the garage and go out there before you have to?"

"Honey, I have my reasons."

"Are you feeling sick?"

I produced a barking laugh to indicate that was not the reason.

"I feel fine, okay? I just feel the need to get settled."

"I just never thought I'd hear that you want to leave the garage."

"Old garage sitters never die, they just go to senior living joints."

"Funny and yet…"

I took a sip of my beer and savored it.

"How soon, Carrie?"

"Well, your room is waiting for you. You could probably move tomorrow. I just need to make a call out there in the morning."

"Make it."

She nodded and stared at me for moment.

"Done. Anything else?"

"Yeah, wipe the frown off your face and wheel me inside. I'd like to sit in the kitchen for a bit before I go to bed."

"Bim, I hope you're not doing this for Mike and I, because…"

"I'm doing it for me, kid. No more guilt or questions, okay?"

"Whatever you are thinking, I love you, Bimster."

"Back at you, Blue Eyes. Now push me in."

"Okay, let's go."

And close the garage door behind me, please."

A minute after we went inside the thunderstorm that had been promised all day finally arrived. The light show went on all night. It made me feel purified. It made me sleep. A lot of things were washed away by that summer storm. Personally, I let it take my doubt down the roof, down the creek and into Winnebago.

The next afternoon Carrie and Mike drove me out to my new home. Room 119 at Cedar Commons was a bright little cell with a view to the south. I liked that because the garage had faced south. Carrie and Molly had been busy furnishing the place to suit me including one of those recliners that push you out to your chair or walker. Although the sight of it aged me another couple of years, I understood its necessity. The bed was draped with a quilted comforter that Pat had made years ago. It used to hang on a rod in our dining room and now it would keep me warm over here. It was mostly blue and white diamonds in diamond patterns. I loved seeing it here.

I had a TV though I doubted I would have much use for it besides ball games and in-house wi-fi, which I definitely would use. There were a few photos hung and placed on the dresser that the girls had dug up. They were pictures from family get-togethers and of course, Pat and my wedding picture from Las Vegas. There were even a couple of artifacts from the garage. Displayed next to the bathroom door were four old Wisconsin license plates of varying color. I think at least one of them was left by Pat's first husband, but he was welcome here, too. All in all, I was very touched by their room appointments. It was going to be a good place to nest. Bird reference intended!

There was a resident orientation given by the assistant administrator, who was a very nice and good looking woman probably in her forties. Good, I would have someone to flirt with, although geezer flirting has an extreme side that I intended to avoid. As I was wheeled around the place I once again was drawn to the large, glass bird cages. I was surprised no one was paying any attention to them, but I did notice as we passed other resident rooms that TV was the main thing people watched. Some things don't change even on the inside of senior living. Well, those birds would not be getting ignored by me.

As I mentioned before, the home has its own pack of therapy dogs (their term, not mine) who were free to wander around during the day. I immediately connected with a collie named Holly, who, I was told, had had a couple of strokes herself. From the first day she learned where my room was and often was there when I got up in the morning and opened the door. I never had a dog for a pet in my entire life and this was an unexpected fringe benefit. I adored Holly the collie.

After a few hours of finding out what was where and chatting I cut Carrie and Mike loose. Carrie got a little choked up, but I assured her I was okay and they should go home. Later I was thinking about going to bed when Sonia poked her head in the door. A second later, the second shoe fell as Des peeked in behind her. No tears here; they were all smiles.

"Hey Methuselah, how are the new digs," cracked Sonia. My girl.

"Any cute nurses yet, Bimster?" Des quipped.

"Most of these gals ain't nurses, they're called resident care associates, but yeah, got a few cuties here."

"Your room is neat," said Sony, looking around then finding a picture of herself. "Oh, I remember this picture. It was from last 4th of July. I like being part of your room, Bim."

"Where's my picture, Bim?" Des wondered.

"Probably hanging in some Irish post office."

"Hah, different place, same smart arse."

We all had a comfortable chuckle before I switched gears.

"When are you moving into the house, Sony?"

"Day after closing. In about two weeks."

"Desmond, what are you going to do with the old Bollander place?"

"We're going to keep it as a sort of studio. The house is still a wreck, but it has historic connections to both Meg Bollander's art and Roland's literary legacy."

"Why don't you just open a museum up there?"

"Hah," barked Des, "no one would find it."

"Just as well!" Sonia added. "And by the way, we have set a date for our repeating-vows ceremony and reception. It's August 14 and you had better plan on making it."

"That's a couple months off, but I'll be there."

"I want you to give me away, Bim," she said. "I want you to stand up for me. Figuratively…you know."

"Yeah, I know," I sighed. "And yes, I would be honored."

Like in any new environment I was a little slow to make friends. Everyone here smiles and says 'hi" passing in the halls, but it is more a reflex than anything else. I am not questioning the folk's kindness, but there is so much of it that it gets stale. I have an assigned seat for meals and I was surprised that I knew one of the men at my table. His name was Larry Oken and I knew him from bowling league. Larry was a fine bowler in his day, but according to him, all the bowling led to back problems and a number of failed surgeries. Even in his wheelchair he is bent over like a switch in a high wind, which makes him have to turn his head and look up to talk to you. He was always a wise ass, too, so at least we got to push each other's buttons like we did years ago.

The other two guys at the table, Leo and Bob, don't say much at all. I got a feeling that some dementia had crept in and stolen their tongues. I hate to say it, but some of the other wackos here can't stop talking and complaining. I am thankful for Leo and Bob's silence. The food is pretty good. The head cook comes out sometimes and makes the rounds. He is a retired US Navy cook, but besides knowing how to cook for a crowd, the guy is a very talented chef. So, my room, check. Food, check. Companions, half a check. I was ready to settle into the routine of growing too old to live.

The second day I was visited by the head nurse to go over my meds, etc. and then I got a knock-knock from the physical therapist. Her name was Ellie and she was bigger and way stronger than I was. She came in with her hands on her hips with plenty of attitude. She went on to proclaim that I was going to have to work for my supper around there.

"I am not going to let you lie around here and do nothing, Mr. Stouffer. You aren't dead yet and every living person needs exercise."

I have never done well with authoritarians, but she happened to be the person I most wanted to meet.

"You gonna work me like a mule, eh, Ellie?"

"Like a rented mule, Mr. Stouffer."

"Well, then you might as well call me Bim as you crack your whip."

"Okay, Bim, you want to get started?"

"Let me get this chair to spit me out into the room and I will follow you anywhere."

Now she is looking at me kinda strange. No one is a willing practitioner of PT in these places. She tried to assist me into my chair, but I shook her off.

"Let's make a deal, Ellie. You won't need to prod me or cajole me into doing what you want me to do as long…"

"As long as what, Bim?"

"As long as you get me able to walk a little before say, August 14th."

"Do you think you can stand up and walk in less than two months?"

"Let's just say I have a ghost of a chance."

Okay, time to cue the Rocky Theme. I prefer the Maynard Ferguson version, by the way. I worked with Ellie twice a day for as long as it took to gain a little tiny piece of my legs back. Holly, the collie often followed me to the PT gym and watched me get tortured, something she seemed to enjoy immensely. Every time, I yelped she lifted her head and wagged her tail. She was beginning to remind me of my first wife, except I knew Holly loved me because her eyes told me so. Besides, I was sneaking her human food from the dining room. Women always love the man who brings home the bacon. Anyway, I wasn't buying her love, I was rewarding it. She's a good girl.

CHAPTER TWENTY-ONE

The thing I hate the most about the assisted living scenario is the guilt that comes in the front door in the form of family and friends of the residents. I have never seen so many painted-on smiles and nervous laughter. Well, it is to be expected I guess. A lot of these folks suffer from two fears. One is that their aging and physically wrecked loved one hates them for committing them to this place and two, that they will end up here or someplace like it themselves. That double play makes a visit to the nursing home more dreaded than the dentist for a root canal. I understand the angst, but I'm just being an honest observer. Thankfully, that is where the therapy dogs like Holly come in. When turned loose on the Sunday crowd of visitors, these animals work the room like pros, glad pawing and distracting everyone like they were sunshine salesmen with bad breath. I have watched them lay their heads on the laps of residents to let the family know that the love doesn't stop when they go home for Sunday dinner. I know every resident home doesn't have dogs, but they all should. And by the way, cats wouldn't work in these conditions just in case you were wondering.

The next two months were long months while I experienced them, but like so many things, they went by fast in retrospect. I had made a little bit of progress towards my goal of standing up for Sonia, but I was still only able to actually stand for a few seconds on wobbly legs. I was like the Great Wallenda on a wire with two broken ankles. Yes, there was some pain, which Ellie assured me was a good sign, but mostly there was no feeling and that was not good. I did get back most of the flexibility in my left arm, which would have been great if the legs worked, too. I was running out of time.

It would have been very easy to take my small gains and retire to the chair. My doctor told me that he was proud of me, but my inability to walk was connected to my stroke-damaged brain. I had heard that all before: signals from the brain to the legs were severed, short-circuited, whatever. I was getting frustrated until one day Melanie showed up with little Roland. He had something for me.

"Whatcha got there, Roland?" He was cradling a manila envelope and he took a glance at his mom before handing it over to me.

"It's the first draft of my book. You told me to write fast so I did, Uncle Bim."

I fumbled a little opening the envelope mostly because I was surprised, but also because I was humbled. This kid wrote a book already at eight years old. I hadn't done nothing at eight besides steal my dad's cigarettes. Okay, and his beer, too.

"Wow, you really did it. Is this copy for me?"

"I thought you might need something to read over here."

"Yes, I do, kid. Our library doesn't have anything except Reader's Digest condensed books." I winked at Mel and she smiled and nodded. "We could use some great literature around here."

"I hope you like it. Remember the plot?" Roland asked.

"I sure do. Space exploration to go looking for God. Did they ever find him?"

"You should read it and find out, Uncle Bim." he said. I sure walked into that one.

"Roland says you have a book going, too, Bim," said Melanie.

"Yeah, I have been pecking away at one for a while. Still looking for those final chapters. I'll send it off to you, Roland, as soon as I finish."

"I want to read the parts about our trip."

"It's all in there. I've just been a little busy lately. Your book will inspire me to finish it."

We did a little chit-chat and I showed them the bird cages and the birds I liked the best. Holly came trotting up as soon as they let her in from the kennel and her and Roland really hit it off. While they played I had Melanie to myself for a couple minutes.

"Mel, I never heard how you reacted to your sister's wedding." I was gambling that this topic wasn't going to piss her off.

"Well, I'm glad they finally made it legal…" Her sentence trailed off leaving some interpretation.

"Love doesn't need to be made legal. In a way they were married for years."

"I suppose."

"Still don't like Des?"

"No, I actually do. I am not sure what my hang-up is. I guess if I dug down deep enough I would have to admit that I was always a little jealous of Sony."

"How so?"

"Well, for one thing, have you noticed that I am the only one in the whole family who is not some sort of writer? In a famous literary family, I am the odd ball who struggles with writing even an email."

"I have also noticed that you are a healer, Mel. You worked very hard for your MD. You can write scripts can't you?" She nodded. "Well, Sonia heals in her way and you heal in yours."

"Body vs soul?"

"Nah, girl, not 'versus'. They work together."

"Oh, I know, Bim, but now even my son is an author. The book is very good, by the way."

"I have no doubt of that. He amazes me, but so do you. You're so smart you could have done anything, but you chose medicine. Look around you: all these folks are still alive because of someone like you. People live longer now because of medicine and the people who practice it."

Mel lit up a smile. "You're a good pep talker, Bim. I love you, you know."

"I know. See you at the wedding, Melanie."

"Yes, the wedding."

I took Roland's manuscript to bed with me and began reading. It is definitely the work of an eight year old style-wise. He just hasn't read enough great books yet to find out how the masters do it. But, the plot is fantastic and it reminds me so much of his grandfather's courage to go places that no one had ever thought of going. Science fiction meets philosophy with a little cosmology mixed in:

The Pro-Ject crew was buckled in and ready for the enormous hydrogen powered rocket to lift them into the sky. Each one of them had a job to do, which kept them from being afraid. In a few moments they would be launched and then they would follow the signals to their destination. The messages had promised them heaven, but the crew was human so they were skeptical and each one had a bit of hell in the back of their minds. Soon it was too late to wonder which it would be because the rocket did not have a reverse like a car. Fire and lift off. It was now in the hands of The Inviter, as the messenger had been named. The President, in his send-off speech had said, 'God's speed." The speed was building, but was it God's?

It occurred to me that Roland had never been exposed to too much formal religion as Mel and Ray were both atheists. Where did his concept come from? *"You should read it and find out, Uncle Bim."* I resisted going to the end and reading that first. If I had I would have missed much of the charm of this young mind working things out as he went along. His grandfather always told me that writing gets better by degrees with each book you read or write. This kid was going to cause a stir by the time he was a teenager if he kept at it. I had to chuckle to myself at that thought. As if the spooks at Ghost Farm would let him quit writing. I fell asleep half-looking for those ghosts, but they had yet to visit me at the home.

Sonia and Des' vow repeating ceremony was to take place entirely at Ghost Farm with the ceremony in the barn and the reception in the house and yard. It was to be mostly a private affair, but I wondered if the paparazzi, with their many tentacles, would somehow show up. It had been a while since the couple was tabloid quality news, but their long-awaited marriage, if it leaked out, might revive some interest, at least in the literary world. The idea that there might be cameras around made me even more nervous about my simple performance of duty. I know when Sonia asked me to stand up for her it was in the figurative sense. I had worked very hard to make the request literal. Now with only a few days left I knew that simple act would not happen. Ellie saw my energy flagging.

"Okay, Bim, what's up? You've been working harder than any 80 year old man I have ever worked with and now all of a sudden you're dragging your ass."

"You're the only person I told what I wanted to do, Ellie, and it looks like I won't be able to do it. And I wish I could drag my damned ass around this room a coupl'a two three times. Or yours!"

"Okay, take it easy. You knew going in that your legs need more than exercise. They need to be told what to do by your brain and those strokes did a lot of damage. My advice is to keep working because you seem to feel better after our sessions. In the end, that's all you can you do at this point. I admire your goal, Bim, but maybe you should aim lower and enjoy what you can do."

This was all good and true advice, but I didn't want to hear it. At least I could wheel myself back to my room. Holly had gotten bored with my work out and was lying on the bed. I worked my way up beside her and we took our nap together. I wish they'd bathe her more often.

Okay, I admit I sulked through the rest of the day. I had promised myself I wouldn't do that once I got into this place, but I broke my own promise big time. I sulked through dinner and when a gal came to put the dogs in their kennel for the night I snapped at her that the dogs were better company than the people around here. That may or may not be entirely true, but I was looking for a fight no matter how petty. By the time I got to my room for the night I was more sad than angry. You see, I thought I had found the real reason for the bird cave quest, but now I doubted my thinking. I had worked backwards to the night I had 'sleepwalked' out at Ghost Farm and, linking that to whatever happened at the bottom of that scree fan in The Black Hills, I was sure it was all some cosmic plan to get me on my feet again. I muttered something about old fools and fell asleep. Before I drifted off I almost prayed that Roland and Garnet would come for a visit. I needed them.

I awoke after ten the next morning feeling pretty good, but then my mind immediately reminded me of yesterday's mood. I was ashamed of my behavior, but I could not shake the feeling of being a helpless cripple. A cripple, for cry-eye! I had never thought of myself in those terms even on my worst days. I managed to dress myself and wheeled out to breakfast. It was Friday and one of the men at my table, Bob, had already left for the weekend with his family. Leo had gone to a doctor's appointment. Larry Oken was there, but wasn't talking much.

"Hey, Larry, you in there?"

He did his head twist and said, "Yeah, Bim, I'm here, but I don't feel too hot this morning so don't take offense if I don't talk, okay?"

"You tell the nurse?"

"No." And with that word he tuned me out.

I asked the attendants where the dogs were this morning and learned they were at the vet today for shots. I decided to skip breakfast and headed to the bird cage, but I swear to God even those little buggers were all perched silently with their backs to me. What the hell was going on? I wheeled back to my room and shut the door on the world. When I turned around I had a visitor.

"That's a nice fit you're throwing today, Bim."

Roland was sitting in my recliner with a halo of amethyst light all around him. I blinked a couple of times and then noticed that it was dark outside behind the drapes.

"You come to play with me again, Rollie? Must be fun to swoop in and goof on the living."

"Well, it seems to me you could use a swoop from me. Save your anger for an enemy, okay. I come in peace."

"Yeah, and every time you show up I get to go for a little walk, right? I don't need any false hopes anymore. Christ! And where's the fat girl? Telling some old lady down the hall she can dance again?"

Roland's aura changed to lime green. I took that as a bad sign and waited for some scolding. His hand came out of the glare and touched my arm.

"We've been friends too long for this kind of talk. Listen to me and I will tell you some things that you may accept or reject. Life and afterlife pretty much operate by the same rules. The difference is my body is gone and so is all that pain I felt. At your age and in your state of being you hurt everywhere, in your body and your mind so you try to grab onto something to ease it. It might be a dream or it might be a quest. You shoot an arrow in the air and pray it comes down in a field of hope. I am no prophet just because I come to you this way. I am only and eternally your old friend. Anything you think I lead you to do is only you using me as an excuse. You are in control and your options are infinite.

"I want to walk just a few steps tomorrow at your granddaughter's wedding."

"I know. You will be standing up for her and standing in for me."

Rollie vanished with those words and I woke up in my chair. Daylight leaked in behind the curtains and it was still Friday morning. I was thinking I must have had a hallucination from the mushroom soup at dinner last night, but something told me he was really here. I spent the rest of the day writing more of this stuff that you are reading right now. I couldn't let little Roland get two books off before I had finished one. As night fell, I resolved to just do what I could at the wedding and let all this quest and ghost stuff slip off me like rain on a peaked roof. I certainly was not going to be the star of the show tomorrow, anyway. That would be Sonia and Des. Cripples always played bit parts and that was okay with me. Then I remembered Raymond Burr as Ironsides. Geez, I wish the stroke had killed that brain cell memory!

CHAPTER TWENTY-TWO

To anyone who has outlived their parents, friends, children, pets, and usefulness, I, Bim Stouffer, raise a beer to you and wish you peace. The path of life gets bumpy down near the end of it, but you've got to keep going no matter what. Yeah, you probably lost your fear of death and your love of life on different days, but they were probably in the same year. You hit the wall and then you have to find a way around it…or through it. We only suffer in old age because we have big, smart brains that are not built to handle despair, but rather deal it out in mega-doses. But, you know what, without these brains you would have missed so much. How many times in your life did you laugh out loud at some joke? Humor is rather complex and needs to be interpreted instantly or it fails. Thank you, brain. Love may live in the heart, but it is born in the mind. Thanks again. Awesome sunsets, fields of wildflowers, falling leaves, first snows are all photographs taken by the brain. Thank you. What I am trying to say is when everything else fails you still have your memories unless some erasing disease has taken even that. Alzheimer's disease is pre-death. I see it all around me and it makes me sad. My legs walked me though many memories, but now they are not working. The brain carries me along with a day and night slide show of everything human, everything I forgot to say thanks for when I was young. Thank you. Better late than…

I think sometimes we are all just shooting stars or maybe falling drops of rain; elements in motion with nothing in common and everything in harmony. My table mate and friend, Larry Oken passed away today. Well, he certainly had a body that he needed to get out of and his last breath may very well have been a sigh of relief. His passing was a topic of conversation for about ten minutes and the he was gone from the memory of the hive. I tried to miss him like a brother, but he was only another falling star to be pointed at, enjoyed, and forgotten. I hope to share a meal with him again someday, somewhere. It is only a hope.

I think this will be the last chapter of this thing I am writing, this book or whatever it is. It seems to have become more of a confessional manifesto of someone waiting for an overdue train into the abyss. I am sitting facing the window this morning watching the weather twist and turn in a gold and black sky. Storm's coming again to wash away the gaudy red dawn. Sailors everywhere are taking their warning. Holly is already on the bed and asleep, her feet flicking as she chases a squirrel in her dream. I learned from one of the attendants that she is fourteen years old, lots of dog years. We have already promised each other to find one another after we get separated by time's end. This is a promise I intend to keep.

So, using a technique I learned from Roland Heinz, the greater, I have written this preamble when you, the reader came to this last chapter wondering how everything went at the wedding. Well, it was a fine, sunny and warm day out in Pipe, Wisconsin and Carrie and Mike picked me early because she was helping Molly with the food prep. Mike, of course, was the wedding photographer and needed to set up. He said the lighting in the barn was tricky, as I would find out later. Since it was a warm day and not a church wedding the dress was informal, which was good because my suits were hanging on a rack at the Goodwill Store. I didn't think I would need one for the crematorium and, well, they were all too big now anyway.

I got to chat with the bride and groom before the ceremony and their excitement and happiness belied the fact is was a re-enactment of the real deal in Dublin. I had a feeling that this was to be more of a wedding than the first one was. Adding family was the key. I would be sitting on the drop-down seat of my walker just behind Sonia and was told I could merely speak my line from there. It made sense and I thought no more about it. Two months of physical therapy could not eke out a miracle. So be it.

I gave Roland Hitowsky the book review he was looking for and he beamed when he got two thumbs up from me. We talked about it in detail for fifteen minutes and he seemed extra pleased that I 'got it'. I told him I would deliver this manuscript to him as soon as I wrote this last chapter. And yes, he was already writing something else.

This wasn't the first wedding held in the old yellow barn. Molly and Owen were married here, too. Roland's museum behind Owen's vet clinic was a natural cathedral with the high ceilings and gauzy, sunlit shafts of light that came through natural holes in the old roof. I looked around to see if any birds were up in the rafters to witness the ceremony, but saw none. I think there used to be an owl in here and then a family of crows. I also wondered if any local ghosts were around. I looked over my shoulder half expecting to see some colored auras in the folding chairs on the bride's side of the aisle. Nothing so far, but it was early.

Gradually, a few people began to filter in and fill the seats. I knew most of them, but not all. Some of them stopped and scanned the display cases filled with Roland-abilia. I felt great pride that I knew the man and called him my friend. Now I was about to give away his granddaughter. It made me wonder who and where Sonia's real father was. He and her mother were long gone in the dust of Darfur, but I had learned first-hand that spirits like to travel so maybe they were around somewhere. Desmond had no family left and his friends in Ireland had attended the first wedding. When he came by to say hello, he told me I was 'standing up' up for him, too. I truly loved this poetic pirate like the son I never had.

All in all, it struck me that this affair was so Wisconsin: married in a barn full of people who had already had a Bloody Mary at the bar outside. Folks who just could not stop smiling and talking with their neighbors. There were a lot of missing persons, too, who had passed away. Harry Stompe, Sonia and Roland's publisher would have been here. Patrick Zeneb, the lawyer who arranged all the Costello's adoptions by Roland was missing. Of course, my wife Pat would be in the kitchen right now with her BFF, Molly. I think everyone except Meg Bollander would have attended. She was probably in the GHA right now loving and hating Roland. There were others, but they were friends of the O'Conner's unknown to me.

Suddenly, Molly was up in front of us and clapping her hands to get everyone's attention.

"Good afternoon, everyone. Thank you all so much for coming. Sonia and Des thank you, too. As you probably know, my daughter and her husband were married in Ireland about 6 months ago, but they want to share that event with you today with a renewal of their vows and a celebration. We are kind of making this up as we go along so bear with us. Getting married in a barn does not bow much to ceremony. I will turn it over to our family friend, Father George from Holy Family. Father…"

I kind of remember this guy. Sometimes I actually went to mass with Pat and this priest always joked with me about wishing he knew I was coming so they could pass out hard hats to the parishioners. It's an old joke, but I always liked the imagery. I think the fact that we were married in Las Vegas on a church junket sort of rubbed this guy the wrong way, but since he was now working barn weddings maybe all that was forgiven.

After a little speech by Father, Des suddenly appeared from behind a stack of rotting bailed hay. There's an Irish joke in there somewhere that I may think of later. Anyway, then everyone turned around to see Sonia coming down the aisle between the folding chairs. She was wearing a traditional Sudanese wedding dress made of brightly colored blue fabric embroidered with gold and silver thread. I am no expert on this sort of thing, but I can say she looked absolutely gorgeous. I looked quickly for Des' reaction and he looked like a mix of proud husband and love-struck puppy. Lucky man.

The ceremony began with another little speech by the padre and then came the big question of the day for me: "Who gives this women's hand in marriage?"

I was about to raise my hand and say, 'I do,' but then something happened. Voices filled my head and light blinded my eyes. It was not a pleasant sensation; in fact it annoyed me that my big moment was being interrupted. I thought for a second I was having another stroke. Not now, I silently screamed and the next thing I knew I was rising from the seat on the walker. I fought for balance and I heard someone gasp behind me. Jesus, Joseph, and Mary, don't be gasping at me! Not now! I looked a Sonia and saw a mixture of concern and awe in her eyes. I started to take small steps toward that smile. It was only about ten feet, the longest ten feet of my life; but I came to a stop close enough to take her hand.

"I, Benjamin Stouffer, give this woman's hand away in marriage to this wonderful man."

The words gave me strength and I was able to turn around. Molly then appeared and took my arm and led me back to my seat.

"That was awesome, Bim," she whispered as she kissed me on the forehead.

I was barely aware that shafts of sunlight had shot through the roof holes and one of them had landed on my lap. I put my hands into the light and looked up to see where it had come from. Several shafts were defined by the dust motes from various holes, but one of them was shaded by a cross beam. On that beam was what looked like a prism rainbow, but I could not see the source of it. Instinctively, I knew what, or rather who it was.

"Such a lovely ceremony, Father."

"Yes, Garnet and you had better stop sobbing before you get someone wet down there."

"I always cry at weddings."

"I know."

"And your friend got up and walked. How did he do that?"

"Bim Stouffer, the Last Garage Sitter and Finder of the Bird Cave, is now a new man."

"Why is he a new man, Father?"

"He left the old one somewhere between that cave and outside this barn."

Epilogue

There was a lot of talk about me 'walking on water' that day. Some said it was a miracle, but some knew I had done a lot of PT and figured I had built up just enough leg strength to move ten feet. In my mind it was a little of both. Somehow I had squeezed one last command out of my damaged head and shouted it to my legs. It was only a one- time thing, but then timing is everything.

Back at the home, I finished this book/journal and went on to other projects, the chief one being stocking the home's library with books that were better for the mind than digests of airport novels. I figured I'd better blow what money I had left before the home got it all, but I also made a generous donation to the therapy dog fund making sure the practice continued and the dogs were well taken care of. Holly continues to stay with me during her days inside and I never think about which of us will go first. It really doesn't matter, does it? Love never dies. Love forever and peace to you all, Bim Stouffer, The Last Garage Sitter.

SPECIAL THANKS
To:

Barbara Murray
Bill Krueger
Jerry Gleason
Fuller McBride
&
W.L. Harris

Made in the USA
Las Vegas, NV
05 January 2021